Blow Dry This!

Stories From Behind the Chair

Hilda Villaverde

Pluma Designs Inc., Scottsdale, Arizona, USA.

Email: hildavillaverde@cox.net

Website: www.hildavillaverde.com

To purchase direct from publisher:
www.hildavillaverde.com

Library of Congress Cataloging: May 21, 2007

ISBN13 - 978-0-9669607-7-8
ISBN10 - 0-9669607-7-7

Fine Artist: Lucretia Torva, Scottsdale, Arizona
Cover Design: Net Publications, Inc., New York
Author Photo: Lynne Ericksson
Printed in the USA

Dedicated to the Beauty Industry....
Thanks for the ride of my life!

Table of Contents

ACKNOWLEDGMENTS

Although we travel alone at times, the journey of a person's life is never a solitary tour. It takes people connecting with each other, creating and sharing the stories of their lives, that makes the trip worthwhile. Thousands have traveled with me along the path of the beauty industry, including my first client, Dee Toci, who, from the very first appointment, trusted me completely. Words cannot express my appreciation for her and for the following clients who have been with me for over twenty years: LaRae Whitehead, Marie Ravenscroft, Dan Gates, Sherry Henry, Christine Sheehy, Marilyn Francois, Lona Jones, Carol Grunewald, Cindy Andrews, Barbara Johnson, Janel Larson, Sally Cooper, Angie Eggstaff, Victoria Green, Phyllis Carpenter, Margaret Gatewood, Vicki Boundy, Barbara Simmons, Joan Chiak, Carmella Ramirez, Rebecca Kennell, and the Fathauer, Rappaport, Wigle, Gaffney, Keller, Bricker, Weldon, Silverman, Falkenberg, Flake, Crawford and Bruce families.

Thank you for your patience and loyalty during the years of our nomadic travels as we went from one salon to another. Space does not permit me to acknowledge the rest of my clients, whom I cherish and appreciate for their continued patronage and friendship.

I am extremely thankful to those who assisted in the writing of this book. My sincere gratitude for my editor, Sue Jordan, whose sense of humor and playful view of the world moved the project along with laughter and enthusiasm. A special thank you to Cookie Kogen for her valuable suggestions, Jayn Stewart for her incredible insight with the proper flow of words, and to Mary Dougherty for her wisdom in publishing.

A heart-felt appreciation for my salon staff, Michelle Walters, Lisa Valle, and Regan O'Kon. You girls rock!

For the Saturday Select Group, Mary Lee DeCoster, Lisa Eveleth, Kathy Joseph, Paul Dickman, Carol Johnson, Patty Crowford, and Arlene Hougland—we're on that bus together, and we're headed for a great ride!

Finally, Peggy Dauwalder, I shall see you in paradise, and we shall play beauty shop once again. God bless you.

PROLOGUE

Recently, a public foundation in our city began an initiative to study mental health in the surrounding areas. Their plan was to identify the pathways that the public uses to achieve and maintain their mental health.

The initiative was directed by a brilliant group of people who reached outside the usual "box" of a medical mindset and asked for assistance from local professionals not normally thought of as mental health providers. I was fortunate enough to have been asked to attend one of several small focus groups that were formed for the study. The focus group I attended consisted of ten diverse professions—a bartender, a massage therapist, a barber, a manicurist, a healing sound and color therapist, a skin-care and makeup artist, a hypnotherapist, an owner of a high-adventure expedition company for executives, an executive coach, and me, a hairstylist.

What did all of us have in common? Is it easier to talk to someone who is focused on a service rather than on what is being talked about? Is it easier to open up to someone whom clients see just often enough to make them feel safe? According to the research findings, these providers of alternative therapies and personal services find themselves dealing with the emotional issues of their clients as part of offering an unrelated service. Clients often talk freely. They openly discuss their problems. The key element for developing trust seems to be the personal connection. The research discovered that these "outside the box" service providers offer a referral system of personal connections with others. They also are aware of the unity of mind, body, and spirit.

This research confirmed what I've experienced for years—that people come to my salon seeking conversation, support, and guidance—as well as great hair! Their stories are warm and tender, outrageous and hilarious. Please join me behind the chair as I *Blow Dry This*!

INTRODUCTION

My name is Dr. Hilda Villaverde. Over the past thirty rich and rewarding years, I have attended hundreds of weddings, birthday parties, bar mitzvahs, funerals, new moon rituals, drummings, divorce celebrations, séances, and some ceremonies so strange that I'd rather not admit I attended them. I have heard thousands of stories, confessions, lies, promises, and excuses. I have been asked for counsel, prayer, money, sex and help in every imaginable area of life.

I am a hairdresser.

Two-thirds of my life I have stood behind the spinning chair. I've perfected color, watched for the best curl, and produced flawless haircuts. A lifetime of hairstyles has passed through my hands—looks that have come and gone are now the new look for the season. Generations of mothers, daughters, sons, and even a few husbands have shared their most intimate secrets and wildest fantasies. The razor and scissors have glided past their ears, shaved their necks, snipped their ends, and moved around their heads like the delicate dance of a humming bird gently reconstructing the center of a flower. All the while I have been observing and listening.

My clients come from every walk of life. Some are highly educated. Others are not. Some are extremely wealthy with political ties and high ambitions. Some have been involved in murder and corruption. Others have traveled the path of earthly saints. I have witnessed healthy, fulfilling relationships and relationships that were so dysfunctional that clients have starved to death physically and emotionally. I have been the hairdresser and trusted confidante to young children and have watched them grow into confident and trusted adults themselves.

Through the years I have become involved in some clients' lives for the sheer pleasure of the adventure. Other times I have felt compelled to respond to their cry for help. I've risked being hurt and feeling used. This diversity of experiences has rewarded me with new people, perspectives, standards of living, and thinking.

There is much to tell about this satisfying career that I have chosen. It is never boring, always shifting, endlessly creative, forever challenging, and as exciting as a Mexican fiesta. I have collected a variety of stories that will make you laugh out loud. You will be surprised, and you will witness what it means to be human.

I believe that we are all voyeurs at heart. We enjoy comparing, contrasting, judging, damning, or admiring others. We pretend that we are not interested, but the truth is, we are! We want to know about the lives of others so that we can better understand and accept our own.

By nature I am an entertainer, and I do this through writing and telling stories. This book is a work of fiction, but my clients over the years have been the inspiration for the characters and situations you will read about. Many clients are now with other hairdressers, and some are in the big beauty salon in the sky. Others are still with me and are nervous that I have written this memoir. Nonetheless, after years of listening, sharing and experiencing mistakes and successes, here are the stories! I have also scattered short anecdotes, which I call "Snip-Its," throughout the book.

My first beauty school instructor, Mrs. Rich, said to me, "Quite frankly, Hilda, I don't think you have what it takes to be in this industry. I don't think you'll last long." That was thirty-eight years ago. Thank you, Mrs. Rich, for your encouragement.

Tammy, Wayne, and Jon took me aside at times during my career, told me that I didn't have enough talent to be in the beauty business. They recommended that I give it up and hand them my clients while I still had some to give away. Guess what? Those same clients, and many new ones, continue to make appointments with me, and I remain solidly booked month, after month, after month. Imagine that!

Please Tell The Police!

T he year was 1973 and the beauty business was thriving. More women than ever were seeking professional advice from beauty experts in the salons. There were fewer do-it-yourself-at-home amateurs. A creative genius—a European hairstylist named Vidal Sassoon—was transforming the European and American beauty industry from what had been shampoo and set to high fashion hair cuts and color. Hairdressers were beginning to call themselves "hairstylists" and were demanding respect for their newly-acquired precision haircutting skills and advanced hair color systems. A typical woman's hair appointment that once took twelve minutes (cut, set, and get under the dryer) was evolving into haircuts and blow-dries that took three times as long. Hair color was multi-dimensional, and applications were more complicated. Prices for hair services doubled and in some cases, tripled. Newly-introduced styling aids and products for home care were the rage, putting big money into the pockets of both salon owner and stylist. Hairstylists were becoming as important as the family doctor.

Some women refused to change with the times. They were older and dependent on their hairdresser for their weekly shampoo and set. Some hairstylists refused to keep these women as clients and gave them to junior stylists.

I was one of those young, eager, hairstylists, and I was grateful to have anyone in my chair. To keep my station in the most prestigious salon in Phoenix, I did whatever it took to make my clients happy so they would come back.

It was a hectic Saturday morning in the salon, no different from any other hustle-and-bustle day of meeting the demands of five hundred clients who would make their way into less than two thousand square feet within a twelve-hour span. Our doors opened promptly at 7:00 a.m. and remained open until the last client was finished. Every hairdresser worked long days, rarely took a lunch hour, and moved quickly from one person to the next.

That morning, clients were everywhere in various stages of processing. The aromas of coffee and sweet Danish were overpowered by the smell of chemicals that hovered around us like the early morning fog on a California beach. The music of Jefferson Airplane played loudly, vibrating the walls, but no one listened.

I stood working on a client at my station in the front, adjacent to the lobby and close to the receptionist desk. From this location, I could observe everyone arriving and leaving. I listened to phone conversations, including directions, appointments, and re-schedules. I heard receptionist gossip and grievances. My station was not a prize. Quite frankly, it was distracting and noisy—the space given to the newest hairdresser in the salon. Someone would have to die before I could leave this spot. I justified being there by saying that it didn't bother me. After all, I hardly missed anything that was going on in the salon. Or so I thought.

This particular morning, the phones were ringing with urgency. Someone having a bad hair day called for an immediate appointment. An optimist called to see if there was a cancellation at 3:00 p.m. Another, whose alarm clock neglected to wake her, was late and she wanted to know what we would do about it!

In a salon staffed with twenty-four hairstylists, nine assistants, six manicurists, a skin care and make-up specialist, two massage therapists, two receptionists, a cleaning staff, and clients walking in the door every few minutes, anything could happen.

Mary, my assistant, was in the back room getting Mrs. Kay ready for her weekly wash and set. I was lucky to have Mary's assistance. I was nineteen years old when I had met her four years before and was just out of cosmetology school. I had been hired to replace her as an assistant to Mitch, a very busy hairstylist. Mary had been his full-time assistant for several years and was leaving to have her sixth child. We worked together for two months while she trained me.

Nine months after I started working for Mitch, he announced that he was leaving the salon and moving to Texas to become a Fundamentalist Christian minister. Considering his obsessive lust for drugs, alcohol, sex with multiple partners, and the fact that he was married, this was a shock to everyone. He left four hundred clients to me, but most of them decided to find someone more experienced than I was.

Nonetheless, I started to build a clientele. Mary's baby was less then a year old when she returned to work as *my* assistant. Her strong body and well-developed people skills were priceless assets in handling the stress of our schedule and the expectations of clients. I admired her wit, intuition, and outspokenness.

This particular morning Mary walked briskly toward me with a look of unease. She took my arm firmly with her powerful hand, moved near my face, and in a low voice said, "We have a big problem." My mind raced to remember if we had done anything different to Mrs. Kay's hair before sending her for her shampoo.

The last "big problem" we had was the day Wanda's hair melted off her head. This client wanted a permanent wave in her heavily bleached hair. No matter how much I tried to discourage her, she insisted that she was willing to risk her hair melting off in the process. Her hair was already over-processed with bleach, and chances were that it would not withstand the chemicals of a perm. The more I said no, the more she persisted.

Meanwhile the Italian Stallion, a hairstylist who worked next to my station, had been eavesdropping on our conversation. He walked over and announced that he would be happy to give Wanda a perm. "For a hundred and fifty dollars, I will give you a great perm with lots of soft and beautiful curls," he said, looking at me for my approval, which I would NOT give!

Two minutes later, Wanda was in his chair, smiling as she anticipated her new curls. Two hours later, the Italian Stallion, his assistant, and I stood over the shampoo bowl where Wanda lay with her head back. Half-inch tufts of hair were sticking straight up all over her scalp. In the bowl were the perm rods with her bleached hair neatly wrapped around them, lined up like tiny, skinny hot dogs. Her bleached hair had melted off, just as I had thought it would. Not knowing what to say or do, I asked Wanda if she cared for a glass of white wine. I thought the wine might soften her first look into a mirror.

To make a long story short, Wanda spent the next year wearing three of the most expensive human hair wigs money could buy. She had a weekly appointment for ultraviolet light treatments to her scalp (which stimulated hair growth), and she received neck and head massages to relieve tension from the stress of losing her hair. She drank as much wine as she wanted and was treated royally. By the end of the year, Wanda had grown six inches of new hair, and the Italian Stallion had spent roughly $6,200 preventing a lawsuit. There was also a rumor going around the salon that he had been sleeping with her to make sure that she was completely satisfied with his services. The Italian Stallion was appropriately nicknamed.

Still holding my arm, Mary whispered, "Mrs. Kay just told me that somebody's trying to kill her. She says they aren't giving her any food or water. She's begging me to give her water, and she told me not to let her daughter see me giving it to her."

This was certainly more than a hair problem. I thought, "Just what we need on a busy day—someone messing up our tight schedule with her personal problems."

I asked Mary what she thought we should do. "Girl," she said, "I'm going to give that little old lady some water. I'm not letting her die on my time and in my shampoo chair. We're too busy for this nonsense today." I knew Mary really didn't think this was nonsense; it was her way of defusing the impact it had on her. Mary started to walk back. I grabbed her arm and said, "Mary, be careful. Don't let anyone see you giving her water until we find out what this is all about."

I watched Mary walk to the back of the room slowly, as if nothing had happened. She stood by Mrs. Kay, who was still lying back in the shampoo chair. Mary moved quickly toward a table by the water fountain and picked up a small, clear plastic cup. Looking around, she poured water into it. Faster than I had ever seen her move, she lifted Mrs. Kay's head from the shampoo bowl and gave her a drink. As swiftly as she gave her the water, Mary threw the cup away. Mrs. Kay appeared anxious and relieved at the same time.

Mary finished shampooing, conditioning, and rinsing Mrs. Kay's hair and walked her to my chair. Mary prepared her for a trim and roller-set. We had our routine down to a science.

As I walked Mrs. Kay back to the drying room, I noticed her daughter, Agnes, sitting under a dryer having her weekly manicure. Agnes was a tall, sturdy, full-bodied woman. Actually, her body type was mannish. Her dark reddish-blonde highlights emphasized her thick curly hair, which she straightened by pulling it back into a severe French Roll. Her facial features were also masculine. Very full lips framed her large mouth, which showed off straight, white teeth. Bushy brown eyebrows accentuated her big blue eyes. Always dressed impeccably in expensive clothes, beautiful jewelry, and very high-heeled shoes that screamed *I dare you not to notice me*, Agnes had the appearance of a woman begging for attention.

Agnes had been a salon client for many years. Her hairdresser was Gino, a good-looking, tall Italian man who had been a construction worker before entering the beauty industry. Gino was married and a grandfather. Although he was flirtatious with the women who sat in his chair, he was not looking for his next conquest like the Italian Stallion. Gino accommodated Agnes's daily 7:30 a.m. appointment for a comb-out and her weekly wash and style. She enjoyed being fussed over and could obviously afford her daily visits.

As I walked her mother to the drying room, Agnes looked up at me and smiled. I had been flattered several months ago when she asked if I would take care of her mother's hair. The owner of the salon had told Agnes that I was the perfect person to care for her. Both of them came for their weekly appointments on Saturday mornings. I had heard through the grapevine that Agnes held a high, demanding position as an administrative assistant to the CEO of a large manufacturing company in Phoenix, and that her family was wealthy and educated. When Mrs. Kay became my client, I was told that she was worth millions of dollars as the heiress of a Fortune One Hundred corporation.

I had actually been to Agnes's home during the time I worked for Mitch. Agnes's husband, an engineer, made jewelry as a hobby. Mitch was buying some jewelry for himself and asked me to come along to help him choose a piece. While we were at their home, he bought several items for himself and a ring for me.

As soon as I met Junior, Agnes's husband, I wanted to run away. He was obese, sloppy, and smelly. His eyes bulged as if he had a thyroid problem, and he stared at my breasts as if he were undressing me. I could hear him breathing hard as he stood near me. Mitch was looking at something on the opposite side of the room and didn't notice what was happening. In the short amount of time that Junior stood staring at me, I felt as if I was being emotionally raped. I was relieved when Mitch turned around to ask Junior a question. That broke the spell and I could move into another room.

I was also shocked at their home. It was dark, cluttered and filthy. Stuff was strewn everywhere. I didn't think rich, educated people lived like this. The house smelled literally like something had died. I wondered about them as a couple: how could a woman who appeared so sophisticated be with a man who was so disgusting? The whole experience was disturbing, and I couldn't wait to get out of there.

From my station, I watched Mary caring for Mrs. Kay. It was difficult to guess her age, but I thought she must be in her mid-to-late seventies. She had always been petite, but now she also seemed fragile. Her expensive, tailored clothes hung on her withered body, unable to hide her dramatic weight loss. Her hair was thinning and getting greyer. Her skin lacked moisture and elasticity, and her eyes were devoid of any sparkle. She seemed sad and listless.

A horrifying incident had recently occurred in Mrs. Kay's life. She had been a widow for many years, but she had started dating Dr. Claude Smith, a family physician and widower. Not long ago, a man had broken into Dr. Smith's home while he slept and shot him twice in one leg and once in the other. A dear friend, an older woman from Illinois, was visiting Dr. Smith and staying in a room down the hall. When she heard the noise, she came out into the hallway and ran into the intruder, who opened fire and shot her three times in the chest.

Bleeding heavily, Dr. Smith tried to call the police, but he was unable to use any of the phones because the shooter had cut the phone lines before he entered the house. Incredibly, Dr. Smith was able to drag himself to a neighbor's home to get help. By the time the police arrived, his guest was dead. Since nothing had been stolen from the house, the police assumed that the intention was not robbery but murder. The crime was still under investigation; there were no suspects and no arrests. Dr. Smith was still hospitalized, recovering from his wounds, and it was not certain if he would walk again.

I considered bringing up the subject to Mrs. Kay to let her know how sorry I was, but I was unsure how to begin the conversation. I talked to Mary about it, and she suggested that I not bring it up at all. Her exact words were, "Listen here, girl, it's none of our business, and we're not going to make it our business. We do hair and that's what we're going to do." As usual, Mary had given me good advice. Neither she nor I mentioned anything about the water or the allegation. Mrs. Kay was a very private person who rarely talked. She mostly smiled and nodded her approval of everything.

Mrs. Kay sat under the dryer, and Agnes, finished with her manicure, sat down by her mother to complete her drying time. I walked over to Agnes and in a soft voice, said, "Your mother was asking for water earlier. May I get both of you something to drink?" Quickly, in a nervous voice she said, "No! She can't have any water! She is on medication that does not allow her to have any water at all. Don't give her anything unless you ask me first. Do you understand me?" I backed away and assured her that I would not give her anything without asking first. Mary was standing nearby and heard the conversation.

Mary and I waited until Mrs. Kay and Agnes left before we talked about the incident. We decided that we would not say anything to anyone….yet. Mary assured me that many times, as people age, they become confused and intolerant. People get on their nerves, and they become fanatical about uncomfortable situations. Their imagination begins to run away with them. Mary had worked in homes for the elderly when she was younger and had experienced some of these behaviors. Because of the trauma that her friend Dr. Smith had just experienced, we thought that Mrs. Kay might just be afraid in general. We would just wait and see before we said anything.

I watched the news daily and tried to keep up with the murder investigation, but my best information came from Agnes's manicurist. She told me that after the shooting, Mrs. Kay was afraid to be alone, so Agnes had moved her mother into her house. The thought of that sweet, clean little lady living in a filthy home with that gross man made me sick to my stomach. I could only hope that her daughter was taking care of her and truly protecting her.

The following Saturday Mrs. Kay and Agnes came for their weekly appointment. They slowly approached my station. Agnes held her mother's arm to steady her. Agnes leaned into my face and reminded me, "Don't forget. If mother needs anything *at all*, come and get me first." Mrs. Kay shrank back and appeared not to notice anything that was going on.

This time, I walked back to the shampoo area with Mary and Mrs. Kay, who now appeared even more weak and brittle. As she laid her head back into the shampoo bowl, she looked up at both of us and clearly said, "Please help me! They are trying to kill me. They tried to kill Claude, and now they are trying to get rid of me." I moved in closer and whispered, "Who is trying to kill you?" She answered, "My daughter and her husband. Please help me before it's too late. I need food and water. Please tell the police!" Both Mary and I knew that these were not the words of a confused old woman. Something was terribly wrong. We had to do something about this situation, and we had to do it quickly.

I looked around to see where Agnes was. She was having color applied to her hair, drinking some freshly made coffee, and eating a pastry. She could not see the shampoo area from where she sat. Quickly, I motioned to Mary to give Mrs. Kay water. I could almost hear Mary's heart pounding as she quenched Mrs. Kay's thirst. For a quick moment the thought crossed my mind that we could be dead wrong and that water could harm Mrs. Kay. I didn't know much about medication, but I had never heard of one that prohibited food or water. I just hoped that Mary and I were doing the right thing.

Mary placed a piece of Danish into Mrs. Kay's mouth. She must have been carrying it in her front pocket wrapped in a napkin—her usual way of eating. I watched to be sure that no one could see what we were doing. Mrs. Kay opened her mouth and stretched her neck up as she lay back in the shampoo bowl. She looked like a young bird taking food from her mother's beak. It was frightening to watch her swallow food that she had barely chewed. My heart skipped a beat, hoping that we were not making matters worse for this sweet little lady. Intuitively, Mary and I knew that we had to do something…soon.

We kept to our usual routine as we took care of Mrs. Kay. Mary and I slowly walked her into the drying room, and I smiled at Agnes, who was now under the dryer.

Two hours later, their appointments finished, Agnes put an arm around her mother and they walked out the door. Mrs. Kay's petite, fragile body was dwarfed by Agnes's large, healthy figure. It was the perfect picture of a loving daughter caring for her mother.

Mary whispered, "She's a lying bitch! That woman don't give one iota about her mama. It's all a show for us to think she's some kind of a good person. Well, she ain't fooling me! I hope she rots in hell, but, meantime, let's get her fat ass in jail for what she's doing to that sweet little old lady!" The police could decide for themselves, although Mary had already made up her mind that Agnes was up to no good!

Every workplace seems to have a staff member who knows everything and everybody. These people are capable of being up on things that are barely on the radar screen for the rest of us. If they're not sure about something, you can bet your last dollar that they will get to the bottom of it and dig even deeper, just in case there's more to know. In our salon that person was Rudy, a hairdresser in his mid-fifties. He was short and wide and built like a storage shed. His red hair was thinning and he had a permanent grin on his thin lips. He looked weird in the leisure suits that he insisted on wearing, but he wore them proudly. He especially liked the powder blue one. Someone had complimented him on how the jacket's color reflected his blue eyes, and the rest was history.

Rudy looked more like a bookkeeper or mortician than a hairdresser. He lacked the flair—the hand gestures, the lift of the head, and the roll of the eyes when he was displeased. Rudy had not mastered the attitude of "those creative types."

No one knew much about his private life except that he had been divorced twice, had no children, lived alone, and had two cats. We rarely saw each other since we worked on opposite sides of the salon, but we were cordial when we met in the dispensary as we got supplies or mixed hair color.

Although his client base was small—about a hundred women and a few of their husbands—they were social icons. His clients were well-connected, which, in turn, kept Rudy well-connected. I don't think he socialized with them outside the salon or went out much with anyone, but he knew a lot about what went on. Beyond his clients, how he accumulated so much information was a mystery to all of us.

It was rumored that before moving to Phoenix from the East Coast, Rudy had been a police officer. We also heard that he had strong connections with law enforcement people around the country. I hoped that he had good connections with someone involved in the murder investigation. Maybe Mrs.

Kay's cry for help could lead the police in a direction that could help solve the murder of the houseguest and the attempted murder of Dr. Smith.

There was no reason for me to distrust Rudy. I had never heard him gossip or repeat private conversations. I wanted to tell him everything, but I would be careful not to disclose too much at first.

After Mrs. Kay and Agnes left the salon, I approached Rudy. He was standing in the dispensary mixing color. I walked in and said that I would like to ask him some questions about the murder investigation involving our clients. Grinning a bit more than usual, he asked what I knew. I told him that I only knew what I had heard on the news and from Agnes's manicurist. But I had also received some information from Mrs. Kay that was quite disturbing.

I began by telling him that Mrs. Kay had seemed depressed and fragile lately, which was understandable considering what she had gone through with Dr. Smith. Rudy seemed to be following me completely. I then asked him, "What do you know about Agnes and her husband, Junior?" He answered with, "What do you know?" I was trying to see how I could approach this conversation without giving too much away too fast, but I was anxious to get to the point.

Completely losing control, I babbled, *IamafraidforMrs.Kay'slife.ShesaidsomethingtoMaryand metodaywhichledsmetobelievethatthereisaconnectionbet weenthemurderofDr.Smith'shouseguestandAgnesandJunior.I believethatMrs Kayisingreatdangerofbeingmurderedherself!*

Rudy calmly asked if I would repeat what I had said. Slowing down considerably and enunciating each word, I said again, "I'm afraid for Mrs. Kay's life. She said something to Mary and me today which leads me to believe that there is a connection between the murder of Dr. Smith's houseguest and Agnes and Junior. I believe that Mrs. Kay is in great danger of being murdered herself."

Putting down the brush and color bowl, Rudy gave me his undivided attention and said, "Tell me what you know, and

12

I will help as much as I can." I told him what Mrs. Kay had said to Mary the first time she had asked for help. I described Agnes's reaction when I asked her if I could give her mother some water. I told him what had just occurred when Mrs. Kay again had asked for help. I told him how she specifically had said, "My daughter and her husband are trying to kill me. Please help me before it's too late. I need food and water. Please tell the police!" Rudy looked down as if searching for something in the color bowl. Then he looked up, stared intently at me and said, "This is great information...this will be so helpful. You have no idea how helpful."

Rudy told me that an investigation was going on inside our salon already. People had been called in for questioning— Mr. Hazine, the owner of the salon, Gino, Agnes's hairdresser, and Zillah, her manicurist. They were all asked not to discuss the case with anyone. They were told that their cooperation was crucial to the investigation and the apprehension of the suspect. It became clear that everyone in the salon knew about the investigation except Mary and me. My theory had been incorrect: although I stood at the front station near the receptionist desk, I *didn't* know all that was going on.

The county attorney's office was heavily involved in the case and pumped our staff for information. One of our hairdressers had been called in for questioning the previous day. A client of hers was suspiciously linked to a man who had just been brought in for questioning regarding the murder. When I was told the client was Diane Warner, I remembered her! I had worked on her hair several times when her regular hairdresser was unavailable. Now Diane was being linked to the murder! According to Rudy, the man who was being held was Diane's live-in boyfriend—an older, out-of-work ranch hand. Rudy called him an "inexperienced gun for hire." It disturbed me that our prestigious salon was involved in a murder case. Boy, did I have a lot to learn about people!

"Do you know anything else?" I asked (as if all this information wasn't enough). Rudy said he would fill me in as things evolved. He finished mixing some bleach, and as he

13

walked out of the dispensary, he looked back at me and said, "Please don't share this information with anyone else. I'll keep you posted as much as I can. It's important that you and Mary don't say anything. You don't want to get in the way of the police doing their work or endangering Mrs. Kay even more. You've done well by sharing this information with me. Trust me. I'll protect you and Mary as much as I can."

Although this was a serious conversation about suspects, murder, and saving a person's life, I couldn't help focusing on that awful blue polyester leisure suit.

Rudy walked quickly to a phone on the wall near his station. His client waited patiently. Rudy dialed the number as if he had called the person many times before. I hoped I had done the right thing, but the alternative of doing nothing was even more frightening. I couldn't know what might happen to Mrs. Kay. If I were a gambling woman, I would bet that Mrs. Kay would pull through and live. But I never gambled.

The following Saturday Agnes called in and told the receptionist that her mother was too tired to leave the house. She was canceling Mrs. Kay's appointment, but Agnes would be in at her usual time. Later, as Agnes sat under the dryer having her manicure, I went over to her and asked about her mother. She assured me that she was doing all she could to take care of her and that she would be feeling better soon. Agnes gave me a cool smile and looked away, letting me know that I was dismissed.

The following week the murder case broke wide open. Newspapers, television and radio stations reported that Agnes and Junior had been arrested and charged with breaking and entering, murder, and conspiracy to commit murder.

The gun-for-hire, a 74-year-old ranch hand named Walter Handler, had confessed to the murder and had incriminated Junior and Agnes, who had hired him. He was inexperienced at killing anyone prior to this incident and didn't even have a criminal record. He had killed the houseguest but not Dr. Smith, who was alive and doing well. The houseguest was not in the original plan, as her death meant nothing to

Agnes and Junior. The one they wanted dead was Dr. Smith because Mrs. Kay and Dr. Smith were planning to get married. With him out of the way, when Mrs. Kay died, the money would go to her only child, Agnes.

When their plan to kill Dr. Smith failed, Agnes and Junior decided they needed to slowly kill Mrs. Kay. This way they would be assured that she would not marry the doctor and jeopardize Agnes's inheritance.

Somehow during her daily comb-outs, Agnes had met Diane, who was living with Walter. Diane and Walter were having relationship problems. Not only did they both have problems with alcohol, Walter had a drug dependency as well. He was willing to do anything, including killing a perfect stranger, to keep his relationship with Diane and to pay for his drugs and alcohol. To make matters worse, Diane had told her hairdresser that she had met another man and was planning to leave Walter.

Another piece of information that surfaced was that Junior had been making illegal drugs in his home and selling them on the black market. As a young man he had fiddled with chemistry and compounds and was putting his knowledge to good use. He was apparently well-known for producing quality drugs.

I decided that it wasn't just jewelry that Mitch was buying from Junior. Because I did not own a car, Mitch had offered to drive me to work every morning, and we made weekly stops at Junior's house. I waited in the car while Mitch went in to look over "merchandise" for clients. I had assumed that the merchandise was jewelry, but now I knew otherwise. It wasn't a dead rat that had I smelled in the house. It was that man and the chemicals he used to make drugs. I had been right: Junior *was* capable of committing a horrible crime. I was glad that Mitch had found Jesus and was now in Texas in his Christian seminary.

Drugs were big in the seventies, and our salon was no exception. Good quality uppers and downers were party appetizers, not only for the rich and famous, but for anyone

15

who could pay for them. Several stylists were hooked on uppers to help them keep up their intense schedules. Others just loved feeling high. The downers were necessary after long hours of being up. That was the cycle of drugs—up and down, up and down. It was all only a pill away. Marijuana and hash were also favorites. In those days, smoking grass or hash was as normal as eating.

Once, at a party that the gals insisted I attend, I watched with amazement as an entire family, including the four-and-five-year-old daughters, smoked from a pipe filled with hash. A large group of us sat on the floor in a circle in the living room, listening to music and getting high. Each time the pipe went around, the children took their turn. That was the last drug party for me. I was horrified by the thought of parents who encouraged their *children* to take drugs at such a young and tender age.

At the salon, I began to put things together. I remembered how friendly Agnes had been with certain stylists and that she talked a lot with some of our heaviest drug users. Agnes must have been the delivery service. As a professional woman employed at a large company and a client at our salon, she came in contact with lots of people. Rudy confirmed this. He always seemed to be a step ahead of the television and newspapers. Through him I also learned that Mrs. Kay had been hospitalized and was under police protection. Her physical examination revealed that she had been near death from malnutrition and dehydration. She had been absolutely right—Agnes and her husband were trying to kill her. However, her prognosis was good. Dr. Smith, who was recovering, had stepped forward to help, and she would be well cared for.

I could not imagine what Mrs. Kay must have felt watching her own daughter on trial for attempting to murder her. Through Rudy, I heard that Mrs. Kay was planning to move out of the state and begin a new life. I hoped that she would go away with Dr. Smith, who was now walking, and that they would enjoy themselves on some sunny beach far from Phoenix.

Mary and I missed Mrs. Kay's Saturday morning appointments. We had developed a rapport with the lovely and kind woman. Her warm smile was a welcome invitation to take care of her as best as we could. Mary and I continued our day-to-day routine as we listened to clients talk about the murder case and their theories about those involved. We didn't say a word about what had occurred that Saturday morning at the shampoo bowl. We took Rudy's advice and pretended that we knew nothing about anything.

Rudy and I developed a close friendship after that. I appreciated his knowledge and connections in the community. I was so grateful that he had kept Mary and me out of the murder investigation and the trial. He was a good man to know.

Junior was sentenced to death. Agnes was given a life sentence. Reassured that Junior and Agnes would be behind bars, I breathed a sigh of relief when I heard of their sentencing. Mary used some choice words to describe her feelings about Agnes and Junior. She also said, "Anyone who would want to kill their own mama for money just don't deserve to live."

Several years after his sentencing, Junior was murdered by a fellow prisoner. Apparently, Junior insulted the other prisoner, also on death row, and a fight ensued. The prisoner doused Junior with lighter fluid. Junior grabbed the fluid and poured it all over the prisoner. One of them lit a match and threw it on the other one. Both men caught on fire and burned to death.

Snip-It

In our fifth year of working together, Mary confessed to me one day that she and her husband were having troubles in their marriage. It didn't take a genius to notice that there were lots of troubles. Frequently, she came to work tired, agitated, distressed, and unkempt, as if she had slept in her clothes, but she never complained or said anything at all until this day.

Mary described her home life to me. Her husband liked chasing other women. Not just chasing, but catching them and having sex with them. He was tall with carved muscles. His arms and legs were long and lean. His skin was the most delicious color of milk chocolate. He was exceptionally attractive. The fact that he had six children didn't stop him from staying out late at night and sometimes not coming home at all. Mary tried everything to keep the marriage together. Recently, she had threatened to shoot him with his own gun if he didn't stop running around. Although it was dangerous to keep a gun in their home with six small children, they had one for protection because their neighborhood was a haven for gangs and a breeding ground for crime.

This particular morning, Mary had come in to the salon exhausted and hungry. She told me about the troubles that she and her husband were having and how she had threatened him with his gun. She also said that he had not been home for several days. That morning she had given her children the last bits of food they had. For her own breakfast, she helped herself to the salon refrigerator that always had leftovers. God help any person who tried to stop her.

We worked hard that day and the following day. The good news was that Mary made good tips on both days, and I gave her extra cash until payday. As I watched her standing outside waiting for the bus ride home, I thought of how strong she was and how much I appreciated her. I prayed for a miracle for her and her family.

18

The following day, I started work at 7:30. Usually, Mary came in by 8:00, but today there was no sign of her. Working as fast as I could and trying desperately to keep up with my clients, I watched the clock tick away until noon. Something was wrong. It wasn't at all like my loyal hard-working Mary not to show up or at least call and let me know she would be late.

At 12:15, while I was juggling several clients, I received the call.

"Mary, where are you? Are you and the children all right?"

"Girl…. I'm at the hospital with my husband," she said in her slow, calm voice.

"What happened? Is he okay?"

"He's going to be okay from the gun shots, but he ain't going to be okay with me."

Quickly I asked, "How did it happen?"

Taking a long, deep breath Mary answered, "Well, he decided to clean his gun early this morning when he got home at 5:00 a.m., and somehow, accidentally, the gun just shot him—three times. The gun just let loose and shot him in the right leg three times."

There was a silence between us as I waited for her to go on.

"The police said it was an accident and so they went on and left us alone. He'll be okay here at the hospital for a few days. I'm going home now to take care of the kids and get some food and sleep. I ain't coming in to work today."

"It's all right, Mary. I understand. How much time do you need away from work? Do you think that three weeks will be enough time off? I know it's hard to think right now. I'm just trying to plan my schedule without you."

"Well, girl, I have to tell you…I ain't coming back to work at all. I packed up the kids last night before my husband come home this morning and shot himself accidentally, and now I'm going through with it. I'm going home to my mama in Chicago. I can't do this anymore. Mama and I will raise the kids better. She done that for her own children, and she done a damn good job with us. Yep! I'm going home with my children."

Then I asked the most stupid question in the world: "Who's going to take care of your husband when he gets out of the hospital?"

Mary answered, "Maybe one of those girls he's been sleeping with might want him. He's lucky he's not losing his leg. I should have aimed higher. The truth is, I don't know and I don't give a rat's ass about him anymore. I'm done trying to force him to be something he don't want to be. I feel like the weight of the world has been taken off me. I feel like a miracle has happened to free me up."

There was silence for a moment. Mary continued, "Now you listen to me, girl. You take care of yourself and don't let *no* man do to you what I let my husband do to me all those years. I love you like my own sister and I don't want bad things happening to you. You hear me now! I love you like we were related. You take care of yourself."

I could hear Mary's voice stall for just a moment, and then she said, "Good bye now, girl, and I love you." She hung up. I just stood there, listening to the buzz of the phone.

To this day, I remember Mary's calm and gentle voice saying goodbye and telling me that she loved me. I can also recall the panic I felt when I hung up the phone and realized that I had just lost my assistant!

A Hairy Tale

Of course I celebrated completing my doctorate in the salon. I had no other choice. Initially, I didn't want a party, but my clients were threatening that if I didn't plan one, they would. They knew I would hate not being in control of the arrangements and that I would be miserable afterward, wishing that I had planned it my way. And so....I had the party. Having the get-together in my hair salon was the most natural thing to do. After all, I have spent most of my life in one, and the majority of my doctoral research was accumulated because of my experiences with my clients. The beauty salon is useful for every resource, reference, and research known to woman.

Friends and family came by with well-wishes, flowers, gifts and stories. They ate scrumptious pastries, cookies, and delicious, mouthwatering chocolate. No one seemed to notice that the day was like any other. Scheduled clients came in to have their hair cut, colored, or permed while others dropped by to join in the celebration. It was hard to tell who were the clients and who were not. Everyone laughed and had a great time telling stories and remarking about my finally completing one more *self-discovery* project. They reminded me that at this point in my life, I had been in school more years than not! They felt a sense of relief, not just for me, but also for themselves, that I would now get back to just doing their hair.

At one point during the day, a group of women who brought along a guitar sang several songs in Spanish (my first language). These women were not professional performers but Yaqui Indian women from the town of Guadalupe. Their gift on my special day was their beautiful congratulatory songs. Crammed into the small studio salon, everyone stood around listening, holding hands, not understanding the words, and smiling as the sweet harmony of emotion poured from their hearts.

One of my male clients, whose hair we were coloring, stood with his head in a plastic bag, draped in a black rayon cape, holding hands with perfect strangers, and swaying side to side as the women sang a lovely tune of gratitude. Ironically, he's a Jewish psychologist, and this particular song was about the teachings of Jesus being at the core of who we become in life.

As I witnessed everyone having such a good time, I thought of how important it is that we celebrate each other's success. No matter the culture, religion, or social status, everyone takes pleasure in a victory. It was an unforgettable day for those who attended, and especially for me. It was just what I needed to end the five-year task of acquiring a doctorate in religious studies, with an emphasis in pastoral counseling.

I am positive that anyone who knew me or worked with me in the early days of my hairdressing career, before I began my studies, would be shocked to learn that I had earned a doctorate degree, especially in anything related to spirituality. These people would most likely remember me as drinking too much, smoking mindlessly, talking meaninglessly, and cussing like a truck driver. They might even recall my appearing brainless because of some of the choices I made. Marrying and divorcing three times, justifying each decision I ever made with the senseless, "I don't want to hurt anyone, I just want to be happy" approach to life, and not having the intelligence to know when to shut up or mind my own business, I did not appear to be the brightest bulb in the lamp.

Believe me, obtaining a doctorate in religious studies did not automatically make me smarter or saintly. While I did come to appreciate that the journey of religious study requires understanding oneself and how the universe works, eventually one does acquire a kinder and wiser attitude toward the world in general, and especially toward oneself. Although I no longer drink or smoke, I do enjoy a good dirty joke, and I cuss once in a while, but only when I'm cranky, hungry, sleepy or frustrated. The story of what happened to me over the years is not a story about one person, but an account of cooperation with thousands of individuals, all freely coming together like characters in a fairy-hairy-tale.

I have heard thousands of clients' stories that have been shared without censorship or distrust. I have been envious of some and have desired the lives of those who have had plenty of money to spend and time to travel the world. Hearing about the purchase of second and third homes around the country and their lavish life styles, I've imagined myself having the same experiences.

During some difficult personal times, I have been humbled by the show of love and support by clients who hardly knew me. Those who took the time to look beyond my hairdressing abilities and made the effort to know me as a whole person have comforted me during times when I had no hope at all. And together we have grown and flourished.

Other times I have felt insulted as I've been asked to come to their home to style their hair for some special event and then been asked to come in through the servant's entrance. Even so, I have continued to discover more and more of me as I've observed myself in every situation and transformed my beliefs and opinions about religion, politics, truth, and the universe, and have thought to myself.... *life is pretty damn good.*

Like many professions, cosmetology is about people. We are a service industry meeting needs for beauty enhancement, personal statements, youthfulness, vanity, self-esteem and well-being. We assist our clients in taking care of their hair, skin, and nails and their outer health in general. Much can be told by the outward appearance of vibrant skin, shiny hair and strong, clear nails. After all, these are the external, visible evidence of a well-maintained inner body.

Aside from the functional characteristics of cosmetology, the relationship developed with each client becomes the basis for enjoyment. Whether working in a high-end salon, a studio, a franchise, or anything in between, I have concluded that most people have one thing in common— they want to be *happy*. If they are acknowledged, accepted, and feel loved, they will be *happy*.

People look for happiness in so many ways: relationships, alcohol, sex, food, drugs, control, cosmetic surgery, money, and endless obsessions. The choices people make to obtain happiness become the foundation of their life stories. Happiness is the goal, and life is what happens with the choices they make. This theory, of course, includes my own desire for happiness.

I began my career in hairdressing with an innocent heart and an optimistic vision for my future. Naïve as a newborn infant, at the tender age of eighteen, I walked into cosmetology school blindly. I had no concept of cultural differences, economic posturing, social etiquette or professional principles.

I was raised in a small copper mining town by poor, uneducated parents of Mexican Indian heritage. Our secluded town was in the southwest desert of Arizona. Our view of the world was created by our home life and what we were taught attending a very strict Catholic school. We children were rarely allowed to watch television. Our time was spent in school or at home with the family doing chores and playing in the Arizona sun.

I began cosmetology school just days after high school graduation. I moved to Phoenix without a car and without money. Originally there were four girls who moved up from our home town to begin school or work. Within a month, though, three of them had returned home, and I was left with a two-bedroom apartment and a year's lease. I attended school six days a week, Monday through Saturday, from 8:00 to 5:00 and worked evenings at Diamonds, a department store on Central Avenue near downtown Phoenix. On Sundays I volunteered to cook Mexican food for clients from the school, and in return I brought home leftovers to eat for the week.

I hitchhiked everywhere. These were the "flower-children" days. Everyone loved everybody, and getting a ride was just a matter of standing on the street corner and sticking out your thumb. Occasionally, the driver insisted that I smoke some marijuana with him, but I discovered that this would probably slow down my progress and could get me in more trouble than I was willing to risk. After all, beer and cigarettes were my preferred bad habits, and they were legal.

I completed the required courses for hair, nails, and skincare in the record time of nine months. I was focused and committed to graduate as quickly as possible. I knew that the sooner I completed my training, the sooner I would be standing behind a chair doing what I loved best.... hair. I also was hungry for food, money, clothes, and friendships outside of school.

The day after I completed my course of study, I hitched a ride to a salon in a very exclusive part of the city. They had a reputation for hiring the most talented cosmetologists around. I had not yet taken my state exam for licensing, but I was hoping to get an interview as soon as possible. My thought was to assist a very busy stylist and work up to the position of master stylist. I knew that being an assistant in this particular salon would give me the opportunity to learn from the best and build my knowledge and confidence.

As I walked into the salon, I was both excited and intimidated. The front lobby was decorated elaborately with gold brocade drapes and beautiful white tile floors. A lush sofa, two wooden carved chairs with quilted seats and backs, and a glass coffee table filled the waiting area. Directly in front of me was a desk so large and high that it was threatening. It was adorned with ornate gold swirls and was finished off with a marble top. A petite, older woman with garish glasses, silver hair and very red lipstick stood behind the desk. Although she could barely see over the top, she had an air of command.

Looking at me with a condescending glare, she asked if she could help me. Feeling totally out of place, and suddenly realizing that I was still wearing the white uniform required by the school (which was stained with color that I could no longer wash out, no matter how much bleach I used), I felt the urge to turn around and run out the front door. But the scent of perms and hairspray permeating the salon caught my attention. I scanned the large room to my right and saw clients and busy stylists. Assistants moved around like worker bees handing rollers, sweeping floors, serving coffee, cookies, and wine. *That's what I could be doing*, I thought.

Standing behind their chairs, involved in conversations, stylists flayed their arms to exaggerate their command of the tools in their hands. All the stylists I could see, both men and women, wore black attire accented by heavy gold necklaces, jeweled bracelets, expensive watches, and fancy rings.

"May I *help* you?" the woman behind the desk asked again. I explained that I wanted to apply for an assistant position. She quickly told me that there were no positions available. The thought of leaving without seeing the rest of the salon just crushed me. As if someone else was speaking, someone with more nerve, I asked, "May I please look around?" I explained that I had just completed my schooling that day, and this was my first look at a real salon. Out of pity, I think, she told me to go ahead and look around, but I was not to touch anything or talk to anyone. They were very busy.

As I toured the salon, I counted twenty-four stylists, six manicurists, nine assistants, a make-up woman, a second receptionist, and a skin care room. No one seemed to notice me as I walked by with my arms and hands down at my sides. I wanted to make sure that I didn't accidentally touch anything.

I was taken by the diversity of the clients and stylists. During beauty school I had become aware of nationalities that I had never known before. In my hometown we were segregated. We had one black man who worked as a janitor at the high school. The rest of us were Mexican, Native American or Anglo. To me Anglo meant white. I had not considered that within the Anglo grouping was such a diversity of cultures.

Now I could see the diversity in the salon. It fascinated me that everyone seemed to get along. Although matters had improved greatly in my hometown, there was still discrimination against the Mexicans and Native Indians. I was glad to be away from all that, and I understood that I had much to learn about different people and cultures.

After ten minutes of walking around the salon, I returned to the front desk. (I actually rushed so that I would not get into trouble if I took too long.) There were now two women standing behind the desk. I made myself stand taller and brought my chin up a bit. I thought I would look more self-assured that way. I asked again if I might fill out an application for an assistant position, pretending to have forgotten that just ten minutes earlier I had been told there were no openings. I made myself look as if I were waiting for a "yes" answer. The second receptionist, a younger woman with dark hair and a sweet face, answered "Yes."

As I moved away from the desk to fill out the one-page application, I was shaking. I thought it must be the excitement of being in such an energetic atmosphere. Filling out the application, trying to calm myself, I looked up and imagined myself working here. I noticed that no one was looking at me. How silly I was to think that anyone could care to look up at me.

With as big a smile as I could put on my face, I handed the application to the younger, nicer receptionist and thanked them both for giving me the opportunity. Minutes later, I was standing outside with my thumb out to catch a ride. Realizing that someone from inside might see my mode of transportation, I put my hand down and walked away as if I had parked my car down the block. I really needed a job so I could stop hitchhiking. I had been lucky for nine months, but I wasn't sure how much longer my good luck would hold out.

Within minutes of arriving at my apartment, I received a phone call. One of the stylists in the salon wanted to talk to me about an assistant position that would begin immediately. Could I come in tomorrow for an interview? (I just knew someone had been looking at me while I was at the front desk.) I was thrilled to receive the call.

The next day I arrived early for my interview. I had not bothered to ask who had been interested in hiring me, which didn't matter much since I didn't know any of their names. My interview was with Mitch. He was tall and slender with a crop of beautiful red hair. His handsome, angular face was covered with freckles that did not take away from his bright green eyes and his stunning smile. He looked young to me. I thought he might be around twenty-seven or so. His energy was exciting and his manner open and inviting.

Mitch wanted to hire me to replace his assistant, Mary, (yes, you have already met Mitch and Mary) who was leaving to have a baby. He explained to me that he had hundreds of clients and that his schedule was incredibly busy. A hairdresser could easily schedule thirty clients in one day. Mitch was at least that busy, if not more.

I was expected to work ten to twelve hours a day, Tuesday through Saturday, without a lunch hour and without breaks, with the exception of potty breaks. I could grab something to eat while mixing color or perm solution in the back room dispensary, but there was absolutely no eating in front of the clients. I was not allowed to chew gum, drink any of the wine that was served to clients, or talk unnecessarily to anyone. I had to wear a white uniform at all times, and the uniform had to be clean and wrinkle-free.

The responsibilities of the assistant would include taking care of Mitch first and his clients second. He was looking for someone who was physically healthy, eager to learn, and had enough energy to keep up with him. The pay would be twenty dollars per day, plus tips. I was thrilled for the offer and simply asked, "How soon can I start?"

Snip-It

L aRae, a favorite client, is sophisticated, smart, gutsy, and outspoken. Her optimistic approach to every circumstance in life has been sinking into my thoughts and stirring my soul since the beginning of our stylist/client relationship that began over thirty years ago when I was only twenty years old.

Her love for world travel and high adventure, her passion for knowledge, and her insistence that I push myself into new and exciting situations has inspired me to do things that I would never have thought I was capable of.

She never lets up. No matter what I am working on, she wants to know how I'm coming along and reminds me to keep a balance of rest and achievement. She is a retired schoolteacher with endless energy, the matriarch of a large, successful extended family, and a devoted wife in a loving marriage. At the age of seventy-two, she is not to be ignored or challenged. The entire family depends on her opinions in family matters and on her insight into the way things work.

Today, while she sat in my chair having her hair styled, I was bemoaning some uncomfortable situation that I had to handle. I was frustrated with a person that I had to deal with and was procrastinating about returning a phone call.

Sitting up in the chair, LaRae turned around, made complete eye contact with me, gave me "that look" and said, "Put on your big-girl panties, and just do it!" I answered with, "Yes ma'm," and promptly shut up.

As soon as LaRae walked out the door with freshly styled hair, I imagined myself putting on *her* big-girl panties and made the call! I love being pushed by her. Mostly, I love her!

S he was five feet, four inches tall and she walked into the salon with an air of command. Her slender body dripped with expensive jewelry, which included a glistening, two-strand, diamond and garnet necklace and matching earrings that highlighted her fire-engine-red hair. At seventy-five years young, Betty wore a khaki skin-tight jump suit, firmly belted at the waist. To accentuate her slender, well-maintained feet, she wore stiletto clear-plastic heels. Her "Bermuda Red" lipstick matched her nail polish that set off a four-karat solitaire diamond on her wedding finger. I had already been a hairdresser for over twenty-five years when Betty came into the salon for a "trial hair style."

"I need a new hairdresser, and someone has recommended you. They said you're good with color and style, and I'm here to give you a chance," were her first words. "You better not screw me up because I can get pretty testy." I kept my composure and just smiled, welcoming her to the salon. (In my opinion, if a woman makes it to this age still slim and trim, wearing stiletto heels and sporting bright red hair, she may feel she has earned the right to be demanding, which is just fine. I'm just waiting for my turn to come around.)

"I hope you know how to use rollers, not like all those 'too good to roll hair' girls in other salons. I don't understand what's wrong with hairdressers anymore. Whatever happened to good ole service and 'the customer is always right' attitude?"

I assured Betty that I was the roller queen of the city and that I was delighted to have the opportunity to style her beautiful, red hair.

"Furthermore, in this salon, the client is always right," I said. (A good offense is the very best defense).

The year was 1991, and for twenty years "cut and blow-dry" had replaced roller sets. Betty had yet to join the rest of the blow-dry generation, but I was not going to be the one to bring it up.

31

She became a weekly shampoo-and-set client. Every week, on the same day, at the same time, she came in for her shampoo, roller-set, and style. Once a month we would also color and trim her hair. Every four months we would give her a perm for extra body. A standing appointment! This is what is known as "steady money" in the beauty salon.

There are only a few of us gals left in the beauty industry who remember the shampoo-and-roller-set routine. I attended cosmetology school back when dinosaurs still walked the earth, and we were required to learn every aspect of cosmetology: hair (which included cutting, roller-sets, perms, relaxers, color, and bleach) as well as nails, skin care, waxing, makeup application, manicures, pedicures, and feet, leg and neck massages. Nowadays, in our specialist age, "hair color technicians" would never consider giving a haircut. They specialize in color and leave cutting to the "haircut technicians." Only an esthetician touches your face and applies makeup, while manicurists are relegated to hands and feet. As for me, not only am I able to cut, color and perm your hair, I can also polish your nails and remove a blackhead from the back of your neck. Believe me, I've done it all.

After we washed, rolled and dried Betty's hair under a hooded hair dryer, the styling began. She meticulously explained how each hair was to be positioned to create her very best look. It was a weekly ritual, and I usually felt anxious as I worked on her. After the styling was completed, Betty stood up, took a hand mirror, and made a complete circle in front of the large, mirror to see her style from every direction. With a slight smile on her lips, she would say, "I think you're trainable!" You can imagine how thrilled I was. She became the highlight of my week.

Betty said very little about herself or her life. I knew she was married, but she never spoke of children or family members. She was very private, and our conversations were centered on her hair. Although I tried to converse by asking questions, she would simply smile and dismiss my questions by pretending not to hear me. I respected her privacy and stopped having any unnecessary conversations with her.

Betty's routine was the same every week. She arrived ten minutes early, dressed impeccably, and always brought a light snack to eat while sitting under the dryer. Her snacks were either an apple or a banana and a Power Bar, and she always brought either the *Readers Digest* or some health magazine to read. While under the dryer, she ate slowly and read the entire time. Rarely did she look up from her magazine, and never did she join in conversations with other clients. She was pleasant, upbeat, and very generous with my assistants who shampooed her hair. She was pleased with my work, and, as long as her hair color was bright, fire-engine red, she never complained, which was a relief considering our first introduction. She had trained me well.

Five years later in July of 1996, I hired a new assistant. Dina was a mature woman, a grandmother whose background was in accounting. Although she had never worked in a beauty salon, I thought she would enjoy the change from numbers and computers to contact with real people. Dina was confident, kind, enjoyable, and very soft-spoken. Betty liked her immediately.

Within the first month of hiring Dina, I heard conversations between Betty and Dina at the shampoo area. I had never heard her speak with any of my other assistants before. Now, I could even hear laughter coming from both women. It was wonderful to hear Betty laughing and enjoying herself so much with Dina.

Over the months that followed, I learned from Dina that Betty was from the Midwest. She and her husband had been married for over fifty years and had no children. They had worked hard for their money, which they had a lot of, and together they had made the decision to retire in our city. They began their young lives working for large companies, Betty as a secretary, her husband as a salesman. Eventually, her husband decided to go into business for himself manufacturing garage doors. Betty quit her job, came to work with him, and together they grew an extremely successful business. They had no family, as none of Betty's four sisters were alive. However, they entertained friends frequently in their large home on the golf course. Betty enjoyed weekly bridge with a group of friends while her husband golfed often with other retired buddies.

Two years passed as I watched the two women talk about everything. While Dina shampooed Betty's hair or stood by me while I rolled Betty's hair, I observed how Betty opened up and allowed herself to enjoy being with us. (Okay...being with Dina.)

Dina was also a serious bridge player, and this brought them even closer together. Their weekly visits also included stories about the perfect hand and the other players.

At some point I watched Betty hand Dina a small plastic bag of chocolate malted milk balls. It is not unusual for clients to bring sweets to the salon. I didn't think much about it because I knew Dina loved chocolate in any form. We all joked with her about her passion for chocolate and laughed that someday she would turn into a chocolate bar or a chocolate chip cookie. What I didn't know was that Betty was also a chocolate lover. Another characteristic of Betty's that I was not aware of before Dina came to work with me was that Betty was quite a jokester. She loved to tell mischievous and risqué stories and was full of tales about her life and places she had traveled. She was an absolutely fun woman to be with.

Bringing chocolate to Dina had become a sweet ritual between the two of them. They would talk about their weekly game of bridge and eat chocolate together. I must admit, I was beginning to feel a bit left out. Then I felt guilty that I had such feelings. After all, our main purpose, besides hair, is to have satisfied clients, and Betty was a very satisfied client.

One day I mentioned to Betty that I also enjoyed the taste of chocolate occasionally. It had actually been years since I had allowed myself to have any kind of sugar, but now I could feel myself craving chocolate every time I knew Betty would be coming in. To my surprise, at her next appointment, she brought two small bags of malted milk balls. I chuckle when I remember that there were six balls for Dina and five for me. Betty said that she didn't want Dina to feel cheated. The good news was that I was now sharing this weekly ritual with them and I now felt included in this wonderful relationship they shared.

In 1999, Betty came in with devastating news. She had been diagnosed with terminal cancer. The doctors were optimistic that she would have a few years to live. They did not suggest any form of treatment. Betty was even more positive and gave herself longer. That same week Dina had been diagnosed with breast cancer and was scheduled to begin radiation treatments. Dina's cancer had been detected early, and we knew she would be fine. We all hugged and promised to support each other while enjoying our chocolate. By this time Betty had begun to vary our chocolate treats from malted milk balls to an occasional chocolate caramel. I still continued to get the lesser amount….which became our standing joke.

My thought about the diagnosis was that Betty would remain strong for a good while and then decline slowly. Dina and I were not prepared for what happened. Betty's cancer spread quickly. Within a few weeks she was not able to drive to the salon for her appointment. She was confined to her bed, and hospice was called in to assist her.

I called Betty's husband to see what we could do for her. He asked if we would come by to style her hair because it would lift her spirits. Dina and I were delighted.

Two days later, when we arrived, hospice had just bathed her and washed her hair. She looked frail in her huge bed, but her smile welcomed us. We talked for a bit, and I saw how quickly the cancer had ravaged her body. Her skin had lost its vibrancy, her hair was no longer bright, and her nails were in desperate need of polish.

Dina and I managed to help Betty into a large vanity chair in front of her make-up mirror in the master bathroom. I couldn't help but notice that the master bathroom was the size of my entire hair studio. Oversized forest green marble squares covered the floor. Large, ornate chandeliers and sconces lit the room, and floor-to-ceiling mirrors made the room appear even larger. A television and stereo system and intercom with security controls were conveniently built in, and there were racks of lush green towels draped over gold-plated rods. This was indeed the largest bathroom I had ever seen. Peeking into the snail-shaped shower (that at least eight people could comfortably fit into) made me a bit giddy.

We did not have the time or equipment, nor did Betty have the energy, for us to roller-set her hair that day. A blow-dry style was all we would do. Within an hour, we had trimmed and styled her hair, polished her nails and applied a little make up, including some of her favorite red lipstick. We laughed and shared our latest salon gossip, jokes, and stories. Dina updated Betty on the latest bridge story with her group, and they laughed even more. It was just what her spirit needed. We carried her back to her bed, tucked her in, and called her husband for his approval. He, of course, complimented her and made a big fuss over her appearance. She was thrilled with herself. As we left her home, Dina and I sat in the car in the driveway and cried. It was all going too fast. We would miss our friend.

One month later, Dina's father died unexpectedly. While Dina was away with her family in Colorado, Betty's husband called to see if we would come by again. The next day, on a Sunday, I went alone to see her.

When I arrived, she was not sure why I was there or who I was. I explained that her husband had called and that I was there to style her hair. Within a few seconds, she remembered me and was happy to see me. We had another minor problem. Hospice had not been notified that I would be there, so no one had bathed Betty. Her hair would require washing for me to be able to work with it. I looked throughout the house to find something I could use to wash her hair, but everything was too uncomfortable for her fragile body.

Finally, I came up with a plan. I took a chair that was made of lightweight plastic from the outside patio and put it in the center of the shower (the one that eight people could fit into). I took my clothes off except for my underwear. I undressed Betty except for her underwear. I picked her up, which was easy to do because she couldn't have weighed more than eighty-five pounds, and carried her into the shower where I sat her on the chair. She looked like a princess.

The water was warm and refreshing. I tried not to get her underwear wet by having her bend forward into the stream of water. I applied the shampoo and began to gently scrub her scalp. Her hair had grown quite a bit since my last visit. A silver band of re-growth hugged close to her scalp and was now at least two inches long. Her faded fire-engine-red hair held only a memory of better days. The suds were full and fluffy. I felt her totally surrender to a now-familiar ritual of allowing others to care for her. I wondered how difficult this must have been for her. Over the years I had seen her as a confident and independent woman in total control of her environment and body. Now she was dependent.

Unexpectedly, she sat straight up in her princess chair and invited me to play "hair-do" with the suds in her hair. Neither one of us speaking a word, I took her lead, and we began to play and laugh like two girls in a bathtub before bedtime. After a few hair-dos and a tiara, Betty bent forward while I rinsed away the suds. Water and suds splashed all around us. She cupped her hands, gathered water and, as she sat back up, threw it up at me. I cupped my hands and threw water back at her, and we began a water fight. More laughing and splashing ensued. These few, short moments were timeless.

As we settled quietly after our burst of play, both of us totally wet, I took a sweet-scented bar of soap, a lush hand towel, knelt down in front of her, and washed her beautiful feet. My mind searched for the first time I had met Betty. I remembered her red stiletto heels and all the other heels that she had worn into the salon over the years, and I wondered how many others who had not had the opportunity to really know her had made remarks about the shoes that she loved so much. I felt a welling up of moisture in my eyes and tightness of deep emotion in my chest. I had an overwhelming desire to kiss her feet, but I resisted because I knew it would frighten her. She couldn't have any idea how much she had touched my heart. I would miss her.

By the time I turned off the water, we were both soaked. She sat, I stood, and on her lips was a familiar smile. Even though the smile was now fragile and tired, it was unforgettably hers.

I took a large towel and dried Betty first. Moving her to the outside of the shower, I dressed her in a lovely cream silk gown. I helped her get to the vanity chair, where she waited for me while I dressed. I dried myself as much as I could and put my slacks and top on over my wet underwear, grateful that I lived in Arizona and that my home was close by. I would be dry in no time at all.

An hour later, Betty's hair was up in a special "do." Her fingernails were sporting fresh "Bermuda Red" polish, and, as we slowly made our way to her bed, I knew in my heart this would be the last time I would touch her. I kissed her forehead and thanked her for all the years that she had graced my life. I thanked her for her patronage, the weekly chocolate treats, her respect toward me, and for the way she made Dina feel so special. She smiled, and in a soft and exhausted voice suggested I learn to play cards.

As I said goodbye to Betty's husband at the front door, he handed me a box of chocolates that Betty had asked him to give me the next time I came by. He reminded me that I had to share them with Dina. I thought to myself that I had to make sure Dina had more than I…it was the way Betty would want it. As I drove away, I wished that Dina had been with me to experience this time with her, but then again…. My time with Betty had been perfect. It was meant to be.

Betty died the following day. Dina recovered from her breast cancer, and someone else filled in Betty's weekly appointment. I remain grateful to this day for the unforgettable fire engine red hair, the chocolate treats, and the friendship I would have missed had I not been "trainable."

Snip-It

Carla has been a client for over thirty years. Several years ago, at the age of fifty-eight, she began showing signs of early Alzheimer's. Carla refused to accept the diagnosis and saw a multitude of doctors. The findings were confusing and uncertain. One doctor said she did not have Alzheimer's. Rather, she had suffered a series of mini-strokes, which left her memory damaged. Another doctor emphatically believed that she had a severe case of Adult ADD. Still another suggested a psychosomatic condition brought on by a traumatic experience or blow to the head. Nevertheless, Carla's memory worsened.

Since she was unable to drive herself to the salon, her husband of forty years drove her the twenty miles each way, walked her up the stairs into the salon, and waited patiently outside the door in the hallway where he could keep his eye on her in case she needed anything…. an unusually caring gesture.

Both Carla and her husband are strong fundamentalist Christians, dedicated to reading the Bible daily and living their lives in a Godly manner. They live a simple life with nothing fancy. They dress casually, drive unassuming cars, and live uncomplicated lives. They are dedicated to their children and grandchildren, and they are a community-minded, quiet, gentle couple (I think you get the picture).

One day while Carla's husband sat outside the front door waiting for her, Carla began to talk enthusiastically about a new, alternative supplement that she was taking. After seeing a variety of doctors over the course of five years, all specialists dealing with the mind, Carla had decided to work with her family doctor. She felt more comfortable with their long-term relationship and trusted that he would watch her closely. During a routine visit with him, he recommended a new supplement that was being touted as a booster for the memory. He was not sure how much it would help her, but he didn't think that the herb would hurt her in any way. Several patients had introduced him to the alternative medication saying that it had worked wonders for their memory and for reenergizing their body. Carla had decided that she had nothing to lose and began taking it.

On this particular day, aside from my assistant Michelle, there were three other clients in different stages of beauty treatments. As Carla sat in my chair getting her monthly haircut, she became animated with excitement about feeling so much better..."Much, much better!"

Carla began talking loudly to me and moving around in my chair like I had never seen her do before. Her memory was indeed improving! She had begun to remember conversations and activities that in the past vanished like fog in bright sun. It was remarkable, even a miracle, and she had reason to celebrate. Her voice grew louder and louder as she listed all the positive changes that were occurring.

And then she said it! Like a European commercial, uncensored and brazen, she loudly proclaimed, "The only side effect is that I am having incredible orgasms! Never in my life have I experienced anything like this before! It is just wonderful! And my husband is very excited about the results also."

By now all ears and eyes were alert to every word that Carla was saying. I moved slightly to my left and looked behind me to see if I could see Carla's husband sitting in the hallway. Busily talking on his mobile phone and writing something down on a piece of paper, he appeared different to me. Earlier, when they first walked into the salon, I had not noticed the smile on his face. He always seemed like such a serious man. Today his hair looked shiny, and his skin seemed to be glowing. He also appeared more confident than I had seen him before. A naturally handsome man, somehow he looked even better.

Getting back to Carla, I noticed that she also appeared healthier and happier. She continued, "You can imagine how happy my husband is. We are having the best sex of our entire married lives.... Praise God for the supplements!"

40

Like a scorpion moving quickly across the hot desert floor, the client sitting closest to Carla rushed over to her and asked, "What is the name of that supplement, if you don't mind sharing it with me?"

"Oh, not at all," replied Carla.

One of the other women grabbed paper and pen from her purse and another ripped a page out of the magazine she was reading. They surrounded Carla like paparazzi encircle a Hollywood star. I stepped back and listened as Carla remembered every detail about the supplement.... where to get it, how much it cost, how much to take, and the best time to take it. Obviously, she was remembering quite a bit. I was delighted for her, and I was especially delighted for her husband, who waited out in the hallway unaware of anything that was going on. He simply sat there, looking out into space...smiling.

Wake Up and Go To Sleep

Yes, I sleep with my clients, but only if I have to. Chaz DuPree was the most handsome man that I have ever met in my life. His long, lean, muscular legs melted into his sweet, tight, little butt like leather seats fit in a Porsche.

Powerfully built in all the right places, I assumed that he looked as fabulous out of his clothes as he did in them. His eyes—clear and blue as the Pacific Ocean; his mouth—full and inviting with a scrumptious smile; his mustache—huge, well-maintained, bushy and brown; his nose—aristocratic and chiseled. All these things made him irresistible.

Obsessive-compulsive by nature, Chaz was great at dancing, soccer, skiing, tennis and every other sport he played. He took great pleasure in friendships and kept a vigorous schedule with lots of activities. As a very successful salesman for a large computer company, he had plenty of money to play with and lots to be happy about. He appeared to have it all, and, at the age of forty, he had dated hundreds of women. He had never been married.

I initially met Chaz through my friend, Fanna, who was dating him. In the beginning Fanna had been impressed—not only by his physical appeal, but that he came from a nice, well-to-do family, and that he had great manners. Chaz was everything a woman dreamed of—that is, until he opened his mouth!!

No matter how well he ate with his fork and knife nor how often he stood to pull her chair in and out from the table, he was always demeaning to the waiters, waitresses, and anyone else in the service industry. When they first started dating, Fanna overlooked his behavior, but as the months passed and he became more difficult to be around, she could no longer tolerate his rude, opinionated, demanding, sarcastic conduct. A well-spoken, highly-educated, and confident woman, Fanna was rarely at a loss for words, but in this relationship she was struggling. She enjoyed Chaz's company, but not when he was being rude, which was most of the time.

However, she enjoyed him immensely in bed. As a matter of fact, he was the most incredible lover she had ever experienced. They had met at a party and had felt a connection immediately. That same evening they ended up in bed, connecting every part of their bodies. They made love for hours until she was so exhausted that she couldn't get out of bed the next day. It was the very best sex…ever!

When Fanna talked to me about Chaz and told me he would be calling for a haircut appointment, she tried to prepare me. Of course, he had a terrific head of hair. He had lots of thick, dark, wavy tresses that flipped and curled around his ears and on his neck, just begging to be touched and played with. Those curls made him appear to be a fun and fancy-free kind of guy. According to Fanna, he *was* fun and fancy free, as long as it was fun according to his way and *only* his way…. *all* the time.

Because he was also very narcissistic, she was afraid that he would be impossible for me to please. She warned me about his demeaning attitude toward service people and prepared me for the worst. She also mentioned that she was ready to end the relationship and was simply waiting for the right time to tell him. After nine months of dating, not even the great sex was enough to keep her around any longer.

Fanna was right. Chaz was a difficult client. Not only was he late for his first appointment, he insisted on taking the time to talk about his hair while looking at himself in front of the mirror, and then gave me specific instructions on how to divide and cut each quadrant of his full head of hair.

I decided to give him the best cut possible, but I would not have the time to get him back into my schedule, ever again. That would be my approach. Fanna and I would have to let this one go.

As he sat in my chair, Chaz told me that in several days he would have surgery. For about two years he had been experiencing periodic episodes of severe, debilitating headaches. They were so painful that they bothered his stomach and affected his equilibrium. After the headaches rendered him dizzy and unstable and finally gave him embarrassing uncontrollable diarrhea, he was desperate to do something. The episodes were happening more often and getting worse. No matter how many aspirins he took, nothing helped.

While he was telling me his story, I wondered if just maybe his not feeling well contributed to his inappropriate behavior. Wouldn't it be wonderful if after the surgery, he turned into a nice man? Maybe that was a long shot, but one could hope. After all, he was really good-looking.

After many tests and a variety of specialists, a neurologist had finally concluded that Chaz had fluid from his brain collecting below his occipital bone at the base of his skull. The collection of the fluid applied pressure on the brain and caused his headaches. The solution would be to place a long, thin shunt at the base of the skull and divert the fluid into his stomach, where he would absorb it into his system. Although the surgery was risky, he had his strong, healthy body and his young age going for him. He would be fine in no time at all, and he could get back to his rigorous schedule (without Fanna, which, of course, he did not know at this time).

One month after the surgery, Fanna came in for her hair appointment. She had terrible news. When Chaz had been taken into the recovery room, Fanna was at his side. He looked angelic. She wished he would wake up having had a miraculous healing. As she gazed at him, she questioned her decision to stop seeing him.

Chaz opened his eyes, and her smile greeted him. They said nothing for a long while, but when Chaz spoke, he was frightened.

"Fanna, I can't move. Get help. I can't move my hands or my feet or anything at all from my neck down."

Within minutes, Fanna was removed from the room, and Chaz was hurried back into surgery. The doctors reopened his body to see what had gone wrong.

It was too late. The damage had been done, and the prognosis was not good. Chaz was partially paralyzed and would have to walk with the help of a cane. Eventually, he would need a walker and possibly, as time passed, he would be confined to a wheel chair. The deterioration was inevitable. Nothing could stop the process.

Fanna cried in my chair that day. What a terrible thing to happen to someone who took so much pleasure in movement. She was also angry with him. The doctors had advised him to stop taking aspirin while preparing for surgery, and she doubted that he had stopped at all. Fanna had also discovered that Chaz smoked pot daily and had refused to tell the doctors or ask if it might interfere with his surgery. Either one of these elements could have made a difference in his ability to better handle the surgery. Angry, Fanna was even more determined to break off the relationship.

In the meantime, Chaz's parents, who lived in a retirement community nearby, were too old and unhealthy to take care of him during his recovery. Someday Chaz would be able to go home and learn to live on his own, but for now he needed help, so Fanna moved him in with her and her two daughters.

I am sorry to say, there was no miraculous recovery for Chaz. He was just as nasty and domineering as he had been before his surgery. Fanna thought that he might even be getting worse, and because she was now angry and resentful toward him, all hell broke loose in their already deteriorating relationship.

Her daughters, who were twelve and fourteen and who were struggling with teenage raging hormones, hated having him around and were angry with their mother for not discussing the move with them. They accused her of not taking their feelings into consideration before making her decision. Fanna's best friend and longtime roommate, Brit, couldn't stand to be in the same room with him and the feeling was mutual from Chaz toward her. The entire family suffered as Chaz tried to take control of his life and Fanna's home. He needed her and resented her at the same time. Times were tough for Fanna, her daughters, and Brit. Overall, life crawled by at the speed of a centipede missing the entire right side of his legs, and everyone suffered from the tension.

Six months passed and finally with lots of resistance from Chaz, Fanna moved him out and took him home. Chaz bought a new car that he could drive, but he did not return to his high-pressure job in sales. Within a few weeks of moving back home, he managed to find a job where he could sit at a desk and work at computer. He didn't like the job and felt as if he had been hired by the company to fill a quota as a handicapped person.

He never discussed his lawsuit or the settlement from the surgery with Fanna and never offered to help her financially for all of her assistance, support, and care during the months he had lived with her. She hadn't expected anything, but it would have been nice of him to offer. Fanna moved on with her life without the well-deserved medal for putting up with him all those months.

As for me, Chaz continued to come to the studio for his haircuts. I made room for him in my monthly schedule and learned to tolerate his lateness and his *exact* hair cut instructions. In keeping with the friendly atmosphere in our salon, each time he came in for his cut, I tried to introduce him to other clients, but he made it perfectly clear that he was not interested in making small talk with anyone. He came in for his appointment and demanded to be taken immediately. Sometimes I could and sometimes I couldn't. Sitting and waiting was not what he enjoyed, but what man does? Nevertheless, he waited, and he tore through the magazines as if by turning the pages in an exaggerated, hostile way, he could get even with me.

Occasionally Chaz and I had dinner after work. We would meet in the restaurant of his choice, I would listen to his litany of complaints about the people he worked with, I would feel totally exhausted from the onslaught of negative conversation, and then we would split the bill. It wasn't the most enjoyable thing in my life, but I felt sorry for him. I was the only one left who would go out with him other than his brother and parents, and those visits were very limited.

Several women from his past had tried to reconnect with him, and the single woman who lived next door had tried to befriend him, but he would have nothing to do with any of them. When he told me about the woman next door, whom I had met, he complained that she was too fat for him. "What is she thinking?" he had said to me. "Just because I look handicapped doesn't mean I'm desperate enough to go out with a fatty." I scolded him and encouraged him to give her a chance and get to know her. She appeared to be a lovely woman. As a nurse, she could help him, and she might turn out to be a good companion. She was single with no children. How fortunate for him to have someone so close who wanted to be with him. Another woman at his new job asked him out for dinner one evening, but his comment to me about her was that she was "too common."

As for his home, Chaz thought he could take care of it himself. Frankly, the house was a mess. I'm sure he had enough money to pay for help, but he refused to spend his money in such a frivolous way. Periodically, I went by to help him around the house with chores and grocery shopping. I finally convinced him to hire a gardener to help with the yard, but other than that bit of help, he was on his own.

As the years passed, I kept a friendship going with Chaz. We lived only a couple of miles apart, and he knew that if he needed anything, I could get to him quickly.

One Thanksgiving Day I received a phone call as I was placing a large, perfectly-cooked turkey on the dining room table. My parents, my son and some friends, six of us, were about to have our holiday meal when the phone rang.

"Hilda, are you busy?" It was Chaz.

"I'm a bit busy right now, but what can I do for you?"

I answered.

Chaz told me that he had fallen while taking a shower and had banged the back of his head pretty hard and that he was bleeding heavily. When I asked if he had called an ambulance, he said he was not going to pay for some friggin' ambulance to come by and charge him extra because it was a holiday. He asked if *I* could come by and help him clean up the bloody mess in this bathroom and check to see if he needed medical attention. After being assured that his front door was unlocked, I promised to be there as quickly as possible. Leaving my mother in charge of dinner, I took off to evaluate the situation. It was one o'clock, and I promised my guests that I would be back for dessert.

I walked in the front door and moved quickly toward his bedroom, calling out his name. When I found him, I wasn't sure what he was doing. As I walked closer to where he was sitting on the edge of the bed, I realized that he was smoking a joint. His underwear was hanging around his ankles, and his head was wrapped with a large white, bath towel. Well, if that wasn't a sight! I gave up my turkey dinner and my time with my family and friends to come and rescue some hopeless pothead!

"Okay, first thing first," I thought to myself. I carefully removed the towel from his head and could see that the cut was about two inches long and fairly deep. It was a wicked slice, and it was still bleeding. This wasn't going to kill him, but I did have to get him to the hospital for an evaluation and most certainly some stitches. As if talking to a child, I looked at him disapprovingly, yanked the joint out of his fingers and asked him what the hell he thought he was doing! He answered sarcastically, "Is it any of your business?"

Stepping away from him and looking at him from the top of his wrapped head to his feet where his boxers still hung, I gave him the order to stay, not get up, and wait.

I walked into the bathroom and saw where the fall had occurred. There was indeed blood everywhere! And it would have to wait. Judging by the amount of blood, I had to get him

48

to the hospital right now. Holding the joint between my fingers, I felt like taking a hit. I wondered if it would calm me down. I was so angry with Mr. Chaz Dupree that at that moment, I wanted to turn around, walk past him, out the front door, and let him figure it out for himself. How dare he call me away from my family on this special day! He was selfish, self-centered, arrogant and inconsiderate. I was done tolerating him.

I flushed the joint down the toilet and walked back to the bedroom where I caught him struggling to stand up and trying to get his underwear on. Shamelessly, without giving it a thought, I grabbed his boxers, now midway up his legs, and pulled them up to his waist. I had dinner waiting for me at home, and my objective was to get him help quickly and get back home to my guests.

The only thing I could do to stop the bleeding was to wrap his head tightly with a silk necktie! I recognized the brand of the tie to be a "Jerry Garcia" design from the Grateful Dead. Now he was really angry with me. First, I had flushed his pot down the toilet, and now I had ruined his favorite tie. He gave me the silent treatment as my punishment. Oh well, he would have to get over it!

Once we arrived at the emergency entrance, I quickly ran in and found someone to help with a wheel chair. Inside, the hospital was buzzing. There were people everywhere with all sorts of problems. People were coughing, crying, and waiting all over the place. This was Thanksgiving, I thought to myself. Why are all these people here? They should be home eating their ten thousand calories of fattening, sugary, delicious food.

Chaz and I took a number and waited with the rest of the people in the emergency lobby. It took an hour for someone to finally call us up to fill out the medical and insurance forms and then we waited again. Of course, he didn't tell her that he was stoned on marijuana, and neither did I.

At last, after an hour and a half, we were taken into a large room with several beds. By now Chaz was as white as the curtains that separated us from the other patients. They had him sit on the bed, removed his "Jerry Garcia" tie, and assessed his wound. They were going to have to shave the area and stitch it up, but they were also sure he had a concussion. Because of the loss of blood, his dehydration, and his medical condition, they were going to give him blood and fluids and observe him for a while. It was now five in the afternoon, and I was sure that dinner had ended at my home. By now Mom had washed the dishes and put away the leftovers. Certainly, my son had left with his college friends to hang out somewhere and watch the football game, and the rest of my company had gone home. As soon as I could, I would call home.

Hooked up to blood and fluids, Chaz lay on his side and waited for someone to come by and take care of the head wound. I excused myself and went to the cafeteria to grab something for us to eat. The only foods I could find were orange juice, a banana, and some peanuts.

"I don't want the juice, the banana or the nuts. I'm ready to go home now. These people are incompetent, and I don't want them touching me any more," Chaz demanded. I reminded him that he was connected to IV's and that we were not going anywhere until a doctor discharged him. At this point he yelled back at me and told me that I was as stupid as the rest of them and that he was now upset with me for bringing him there.

Aware that the rest of the beds were occupied and that only a curtain separated us from other patients, I became embarrassed and asked him to calm down and not make a scene. As if I had added gasoline to a fire, he started yelling and calling me names. He tried to get up from the bed but was too weak to do so. A nurse came in, helped me lay him back down, and asked me if I was okay. I assured her that I was fine, but that I was about to kill my ungrateful friend.

She gently took his hand and tried to get him to be patient. She explained that there had been a terrible emergency and they were all as busy as could be. Assuring him that he was not in any danger, she hoped to calm him, but her

50

assurance did not stop him. His voice became louder and louder as he insisted that the hospital was responsible for his ill health and that he was not going to put up with them any longer. Chaz was making a complete fool of himself, and I was sure that everyone in the entire hospital could hear him.

I sat watching him and thought, "What have I gotten myself into? I should have dumped his now-skinny ass when Fanna did years ago." By now, she had met someone else and was getting married, a fact I had not shared with Chaz. She had been smart to dump him when she did.

The nurse left the room and within minutes came back with a small bottle of liquid that she added to the fluid he was receiving. She bent down, put her face up against his, and through tightened teeth said, "Listen here, you selfish idiot. Two young boys were brought in minutes ago with gunshot wounds to their bellies, and we're about to lose them. You're an inconsiderate, arrogant person. Now you lie here and shut up until I can get back to you. Do you understand me?"

Chaz quieted down and closed his eyes. I left his bedside and found a phone in the lobby to call my mother. It was now nine o'clock, and it would be a while before we could leave.

An hour passed before I came back to sit with Chaz. He had calmed down considerably. It must have been that little *treat* the nurse had added to his fluids. A few minutes later, a different nurse came in and shaved and prepared the back of his head. Next, the doctor who had examined him earlier came in, stitched up the cut, and bandaged his head.

I sat and watched as Chaz finally fell into a deep sleep. Every fifteen minutes or so the nurse would come in and wake him and then ask him to go back to sleep, which he did.

At midnight I called my mother again to let her know that we were on our way home. I said "we" because the doctor insisted that Chaz not be left alone. He would have to spend the night with me, in my bed, so that every couple of hours I could wake him up and make sure he was doing well.

Sleepy and slightly drugged, Chaz did not know what the plan was when the nurse helped me get him into my car. We drove home in silence. When he realized that we had arrived at my home, he demanded to know why I had not taken him to his house. I explained to him that the doctor did not want him left alone, and I was not going to spend the night at his house when my parents were waiting for me at mine. He was too tired to argue. Thank God!

Although it had been hours since Thanksgiving dinner had been served, consumed, and put away, I could still smell the aroma of everything as we walked into the kitchen from the garage. Chaz went ahead of me with the help of his walker, and I stayed close behind him and held on to the back of his pants to steady him. With great effort, dragging his feet with each step, he moved past the kitchen and into the dining room where I knew Mom would be sitting working on a picture puzzle.

"Mom, this is Chaz Dupree." I said as we stood facing her. His head bent down, somewhat embarrassed. I continued, "Chaz is sleeping in my bed with me tonight. Is that all right with you?" She knew I was trying to embarrass him even further, if there was such a place for him to go.

In her broken English, she played the game along with me and answered, "It's up to you. You do what you have to do. I not go to bed tonight. I wait here until the morning."

I pointed in the direction of my bedroom, and Chaz took the lead again. I followed close behind, holding on to him by his pants. His body was feeling heavier. He must have been exhausted. Not one word was said as I undressed him down to his boxers. I tucked him into bed and went back to the dining room to have dinner.

Mom pushed puzzle pieces around on the dining room table, my step-dad slept in the front bedroom, and I ate an entire Thanksgiving dinner, including pie. I could hear Chaz snoring in the other room and made a comment to Mom that it would be a very long night!

It was two in the morning when I crawled into bed next to Chaz. I wondered if I still had to wake him up if he was sleeping so soundly—and loudly.

"Chaz, wake up." I shook him a bit and asked him again, "Chaz, wake up." He opened his eyes and looked at me with no expression. "Wake up and go to sleep."

I rolled over, fell asleep, and did not wake up until the sun came in through the bedroom window. Startled, I realized that I had not been awake to wake Chaz. Looking at the alarm clock, I saw that it was after seven. I rolled over to face him. His eyes were closed and he lay very still. "Wake up, Chaz," I said as I shook him. Slowly he opened his eyes and looked at me. "I'm awake," he answered, "and I wet your friggin' bed."

That was the last day I spent time with Chaz Dupree. I didn't hear from him after I took him home and cleaned up the blood from the bathroom, but I did hear from Fanna that he was getting along fine. She had called him to let him know she was getting married, and he told her that he really didn't give a damn what she did with her life.

Snip-It

Laura called today and said she had *bad news* and *really bad news*. When I asked her to give me the *really* bad news first, she answered, "I have to cancel my hair appointment for Wednesday next week."

"Okay," I responded, "and what is the bad news?"

She replied, "The bad news is that the doctor thinks I have uterine cancer and wants me to have a hysterectomy on Wednesday. But maybe I could have the hysterectomy on Monday and still come to the salon for my appointment on Wednesday!"

Now that is a loyal client!!

Things Aren't Always What They Seem

In 1984 the talk of the town around the hairdressers' gossip mill was a newly-opened, exclusive, very expensive hair salon in the heart of downtown Scottsdale. Camelot was its name, and not only was it portrayed as an elite salon where the menu of services included the usual hair, nail, skin care, and makeup accoutrements, but also boasted many extras, including body massage for both women and men, a men's private booth barber shop with a shoe shine stand, sauna, Jacuzzi tubs, showers, locker rooms, cellulite treatments, wine, beer, snacks, and a limo service for transportation to and from the salon. Local newspaper articles compared Camelot to the illustrious *Elizabeth Arden's Red Door Salon* in Phoenix. Other articles also bragged that Camelot would be the number one choice for those clients who demanded exceptional, luxurious pampering!

I received a call from a friend who invited me to visit Camelot with her. She was considering making a change to a different salon and wanted to see if it was as wonderful as everyone was saying. I was unhappy working at my current salon and decided to join her, just to see what they had to offer. To our amazement, it *was* absolutely beautiful. Upon entering the double doors of the two-story building, we were immediately impressed by the elegance of a spacious lobby with white and peach mosaic marble floors.

A large mahogany desk took up the entire wall on the left with enough room to accommodate several receptionists, numerous telephones, and an oversized appointment book. In the center of the lobby an array of colorful, fresh flowers sat on a round, wood carved antique table, adding even more ambience to the spectacular entrance. On the opposite side of the desk was a women's clothing boutique with negligees and

55

sexy underwear as specialty items. "Nice touch," we both said at the same time as we walked into the boutique.

One of the receptionists who had been standing behind the desk came up to us and offered to give us a tour of the salon. She had that "Vanna White" (hostess of a television game show) look about her. Young, blonde, and beautiful, she walked and talked with an air of confidence. Holding her head straight up from her long outstretched neck, she moved with grace and perfect posture. While turning her entire body as though it might break if she moved the wrong way, she pointed with her hand toward a doorway and smiled at us graciously as we left the lobby and entered a hallway just past the reception desk.

We walked into the men's barbershop, which included the shoeshine stall we had read about in the newspaper article. Opposite the barbershop were the men's and women's spa accommodations. Vanna went on to explain, "There are two separate areas, both exactly the same size, equipped with massage tables, Jacuzzi tub, sauna, dressing room, restrooms, and a sitting area for resting between treatments. There are plenty of plush towels, dressing gowns, and a refrigerator with a selection of imported beer, wine, cheese and crackers. Our goal is to create an atmosphere of lavish self-indulgence."

As we exited the women's spa and continued down the hall, we came to the end of the floor where there were two doors. She explained that the door to our left was the salon office, and we would not be entering. The door in front of us was the dispensary. No bigger than a small walk-in closet, it was stocked with all the products and supplies used in the salon, including perms, colors, massage oils, cuticle creams, bobby pins, cotton balls, gloves, paper towels, formaldehyde liquid and tablets, and an entire arsenal of skin care paraphernalia. Everything was neatly organized and labeled on shelves that lined the room from top to bottom. This, I thought, must be the work of someone who really loves detail…and doesn't have a personal life outside this building.

While assessing the inventory of the dispensary, Vanna, whose name we now knew was Valerie, was paged over the intercom to return to the front desk. She asked us to wait for her, assuring us that she would return quickly to continue the tour. When she left, our curiosity got the best of us, and we peeked into the barely open door next to the dispensary. No bigger than nine feet by nine feet, the office was jammed with two inexpensive steel desks, both facing the door. The desks were covered with paperwork, product samples, empty food containers and unopened mail. Filing cabinets lined the walls. Shelves had been built above the cabinets. On the smaller of the two desks sat a computer. I had heard that someday, not only every business, but every home would have a computer, but I couldn't imagine what it would be used for. I remember thinking that I would never have any use for such a frivolous toy! Surprisingly, the office was out of place from the rest of the salon. It was messy and cluttered—the opposite of what we had seen so far. Valerie reappeared, and we were off to continue our tour.

On the upstairs floor was a second lobby. It was not as spacious as the one downstairs, but it was beautifully decorated and comfortable. Spectacular workstations on either side of the sitting area held twenty-five stylists, assistants, and at least eight manicurists. Private rooms for facials and hair removal treatments and well-lit make-up stations were placed toward the back of the spacious room. The shampoo room had ten bowls and gorgeous, leather chairs that easily reclined to accommodate any size person. Never had I seen such attention given to the design and flow of a work area. Everything had been custom-built to meet the needs of both clients and staff.

In addition to the upstairs lobby and work areas, there was an employee lounge with a standard size refrigerator, microwave, coffeemaker, utensils, and tables with chairs. Okay, so this really pulled at our heartstrings. Neither one of us had ever worked in a salon where we could sit and eat. This last room was a great way for us to complete our tour. Valerie led us back downstairs and graciously invited us back anytime we wanted.

Camelot was the most beautiful salon either of us had ever seen. It surpassed our expectations. *Bravo!* I thought to myself. A great group of people must have created this salon.

After visiting Camelot, it was difficult for me to continue working at Prime Time. When I had begun working there, the owner was Bobbie Bell, an easy-going, warm, generous woman. She had been in the beauty industry for over twenty years, was knowledgeable about service and client retention, and understood the importance of taking care of her staff.

As her employee, I appreciated that she handled all the details that made the salon run smoothly. Bobbie divided her time between working on clients as a hairdresser and managing as the owner. The salon was small: four hairdressers, two manicurists, and a skin care specialist. Although I am sure there were challenges in running the business, Bobbie never talked about problems and simply took care of things. She was a terrific boss, and her example of cooperation and respect for others carried over in the way we all got along.

Bobbie's husband was an ambitious, hard-working man. One year after I started working for her, Bobbie's husband hit the jackpot with a new business he was creating. They became millionaires overnight. Well, not quite overnight, but it seemed like it to me. Within weeks, Bobbie had sold the salon and left us to new owners.

A Greek couple purchased the salon for their twenty-year-old daughter, who had recently graduated from cosmetology school. The father, Mr. Danas, was retired and needed something to keep him busy. He thought the salon would be a diversion for him and a good investment in his daughter's future. We didn't know what career Mr. Danas had retired from, but after a few months we surmised that he had been a dictator on a small Greek Island. He was a tyrant. Every afternoon toward the end of our workday, he would burst through the front door, arrogantly announcing his arrival. He would spend the next hour looking over the books to see what we had accomplished, always remarking that it wasn't enough to make the monthly expenses.

The mother, Mrs. Danas, was a frightened and passive woman who literally shook when her husband entered the room. She worked the reception desk, welcomed the clients, answered the phone, and scheduled appointments. She was pleasant, but her demeanor was nervous and guarded. She reminded us of a neglected, attention-craving poodle.

When the six staff members of Prime Time had met with the Danas family for the first time, we thought they would be competent and caring and continue the high standard of professionalism and service that Bobbie had set in place. But we couldn't have been more wrong.

My sister, Maggie, an assistant at the salon, had questioned their integrity from the beginning. I suggested to her that just because Mrs. Danas was missing her two front teeth it did not mean they were not well-intentioned people. Maggie said, "I don't trust him. A good husband would have his wife's teeth fixed. He would not ignore something so important. If he treats her that way, he will treat us worse. Not only that, she deserves it! After all, she has been married to that dictator for almost forty years." Maggie would then break out into a chorus of "All I Want for Christmas is My Two Front Teeth."

Their daughter, Athena (appropriately named for her wisdom, according to her parents), was clueless as to how to manage the salon. She was immature, impetuous, and spoiled. But her father was totally taken by her and succumbed to anything she asked for, especially if he saw the mere hint of a tear in her eye.

During the time we worked for the Danas family, Athena was planning her wedding. Hour after hour, she and her mother lingered over bridal magazines at the front desk. Any disruption by client or staff was regarded as a huge inconvenience. Athena, who was tall, slender and very pretty, would look down at the intruder as though a major violation had occurred. It was hard to tolerate Mr. Danas, the dictator, his exhausting wife, and Athena's self-importance. Not to mention the fact that Maggie was wearing us down singing

Christmas songs in July!

Nine months after I visited Camelot, the Danas family helped finalize my decision to leave. The decision came after discovering that Mr. Danas, who had started an employee retirement fund and was deducting a percentage from our weekly paychecks, had used the funds for something else. He refused to tell us where the money had gone, but he promised that within a year the money would be replaced. Maggie had a gut feeling that the money was being used to fund Athena's wedding. Although it was a small amount that we had contributed thus far, the fact that he had lied to us and the fact that it was illegal was enough to send us packing.

At the same time, while all of this was happening with the Danas regime, my personal life was a disaster. I had been married five years to my second husband, and our marriage was falling apart. When I first met my husband, I was attracted to his outgoing, optimistic personality and sense of humor. He had an enormous amount of energy, was intelligent and handsome, and was a take-charge kind of person with a commanding presence.

After a six-month courtship, we moved quickly into the next stage of our relationship, and he insisted that we marry as soon as possible. After all, I was almost thirty, and he was thirty-five. We obviously knew what we were doing.

His affluent lifestyle and position as vice-president of a very successful company enticed me into envisioning a comfortable life for my son and me. A large home in an exclusive, desirable neighborhood, expensive cars, and shopping trips to La Jolla, California, became my new standard of living. My son attended private school, and I wore a diamond wedding ring that cost more than my home had in my previous marriage.

The company he worked for owned a yacht in San Diego, a ten-passenger jet that was used for transporting and entertaining clients, a home in the mountains, and a number of other benefits that we had the privilege of enjoying. Our lives were filled with entertaining, travel, and material consumption.

My clients were excited when I married him. I had been a single mother raising my son, and they thought it would be good for both of us to have a well-to-do, stable man in our lives. It was a marriage made in heaven—or so we thought.

Within a year of our wedding day, I knew that something terrible was happening to our marriage. My husband became adamant that he be notified of *everything* that was happening in our home. No matter how trivial it was, he wanted to be part of it. From scheduling the housekeeper, gardener, handyman, pest-control man, and window washer, he had to know the exact times when they would arrive and leave. When he arrived home after work, he inspected the house to see what had been done in his absence. If things were not to his liking, he would do them over again, complaining the entire time. This process included re-vacuuming the carpeting in the whole house and re-mowing the lawn, front and back. Insisting that he simply wanted things done right and that he was trying to teach me how to run the house better, he controlled our lives completely.

Then he began taking away my personal freedoms. I had to be available for his phone calls, lunches on my days off, business dinners, company trips, and events that he deemed important. Although I had a new car when we first married, he demanded that I now drive a newer, bigger, better car. My son had to attend the private school of his choosing, and from now on he would buy all of my clothes. If I was late from the grocery store, he wanted a full report as to who I saw and why it took so long. Going out with my girlfriends was out of the question. My life was to be dedicated to his career. His insistence on my quitting my job became a daily argument and a major frustration. He apparently believed that my job as a hairdresser was beneath his image of himself. He argued that it took too much time out of my schedule, and he wanted my complete attention as he climbed the ladder of success. I refused to stop working entirely and scheduled myself to work three days a week. This way I could keep up with my clients and have my own money to spend. I had an intuitive feeling that I shouldn't give up my career completely. Somehow, even though I hadn't given *all* my attention to his career, on our second anniversary he was promoted to president of the company.

We settled into a routine of trying to juggle his schedule, my work, home responsibilities, and my son's school and after-school sports and activities. We kept a very busy schedule of social activities, entertaining, and trying to keep up with the neighbors. This was a new game for me, one I had never played before. His insistence on keeping up an affluent important image kept me in a state of constant stress and anxiety. Pretending, pretending, and more pretending!

Just before our fifth anniversary, my husband came home one evening and announced that he had quit his job as president of the company. He did not want to discuss it. He went around the house gathering clothes, writing paper, blankets, books, food and a small television set and announced that he would be spending time locked up in the front bedroom. Before going in, he stipulated that I was not to knock on the door or bother him. He said he would come out when he was good and ready and that he absolutely did not want to be disturbed by anyone.

He slammed the door shut and locked it. Several days later, no matter what I did or said through the locked door, he would not answer. At first I tried to reason with him by telling him that it scared me not knowing if he was okay. Then I became angry and banged on the door and demanded that he not do such a stupid and ridiculous thing to us. But nothing worked. Not a sound came from the room. I finally walked away and decided that I would wait for it to start smelling and then I would call the police. "Screw him!" I thought to myself. "If he wants to act like a spoiled child without any thought to his responsibilities, I'm not going to stop him. I might enjoy the peace and quiet around the house." Thank God there was a bathroom with a shower connected to his new bedroom.

We did not see him for months, but I knew he was eating daily. I left food in the refrigerator and on the kitchen counter when I left for work in the morning, and it would be gone when I returned. On weekends, I would loudly announce by his locked door that my son and I were leaving for a while, and the same thing would happen. Leave it to a man not to skip a meal!

I could tell that he was showering and shaving. He was fastidious, and I found clothes in the hamper on a regular basis. I was beginning to get the feeling that this was not the first time he had engaged in a vanishing act.

The household bills were steadily coming in, and I tried to keep up as much as I could. I made sure all payments pertaining to our home were current, but I also knew that I needed help if I was going to keep us afloat. Although he had a very good income, we lived a high life style. There was nothing that we wanted for. Our lives had become a manic version of consumerism. Owning a lovely home in the neighborhood was not enough. It had to be the *best* house in the neighborhood. We had to have the best clothing, the newest cars, the biggest everything! He was unstoppable, and now *I* was paying for it. As I opened the monthly bills, I saw that our affluent lifestyle had been paid for with credit cards and home equity loans.

On the fifth month of his lock-up, I made the decision to leave Prime Time Salon and the Danas family to accept a hairstyling position with Camelot. I had no idea how long he would remain locked up or how he would feel after coming out, but I needed to prepare myself for anything. I was sick and tired of lying to my family, friends, and neighbors about his absence. I should have made the decision to leave him at this time, but making one major decision seemed enough for me then.

On a Sunday afternoon, while my son and I were sitting at the kitchen table about to have dinner, my husband emerged from the room after six months of seclusion. He behaved as though he had only been napping. My son excused himself after dinner, and we began talking.

My husband said that after much thought, he had decided to change careers and start a new business. He wanted to know how much was left in our savings and checking accounts. What was our current financial picture? Had I charged anything on credit cards, and had there been any unexpected expenses while he was *unavailable*? As if nothing had happened, he went through the paperwork from our household files and announced that he had prepared a business plan for his new venture. There were charts estimating the time, expenses and capital needed to successfully reach his desired income. Having built successful businesses before, without a doubt he could do it again. Of course, my financial support would be expected, and it was at this point in our conversation that I told him about my move to Camelot. He was very pleased.

Taking advantage of his new, agreeable mood, I said that if we did not get marriage counseling and he continued with his severe mood swings, I would be forced to leave. I would help him financially as much as I could, but I needed to have an intimate partnership with him. I wanted a husband, not just a financial colleague. He agreed, and we found a counselor that we both liked. We began the process of re-constructing our marriage.

A couple of months into counseling, the therapist recommended psychological testing for him. Aside from being a brilliant man, handsome, blah, blah, blah… he was diagnosed with bipolar disorder and obsessive-compulsive disorder and a few side-effects of these mental disorders that I refuse to talk about at this point. I already feel stupid for not paying attention to the big red flags that I should have paid attention to while we were dating. Enough said!

The diagnosis made sense and gave me a basis from which to manage my own feelings and thoughts. I could now begin making choices for myself and not feel responsible for his happiness. Making him happy was no longer my responsibility. His moods swings had been like bed sheets flapping on a clothes line during a Category-4 hurricane. Now

I would at least know when to bring in my own bed sheets before the storm hit. The thought crossed my mind that if he was so brilliant, let him deal with his own sheets. And just like any devastating hurricane, the aftermath of our dysfunctional years together was going to take time to clean up and rebuild.

After his analysis, he began taking medication. Relieved, I could see signs of his settling into a calmer temperament. I began to enjoy him again. We were having conversations, going out for dinner, movies, and concerts, even traveling to California for a romantic holiday. He began paying attention to my son and was participating in his activities again. We also purchased a new home in Scottsdale, which was less then five minutes from Camelot. Our relationship appeared to be recovering. I found myself feeling as if I could trust him again.

Unfortunately, the medication and his composed manner didn't last long. Within a few short months after moving into our new home, he refused to take the medication, claiming that it made him feel uneasy, bloated and fat. I tried to convince him to talk to the doctor, but he was too busy doing the next thing toward his new business. Insisting that he could manage his moods and obsessions without the medication, I could do or say nothing to persuade him otherwise. In his determined *"Don't bother me with that stuff. I've got things to do,"* manner, he plowed forward, convinced he could handle it all. There would be no more counseling or medication, and that was the end of that conversation. I could sense the mania and the obsessive disorder creeping in like a thief coming to steal my happiness.

Before I had started working at Camelot, I went by to fill out some paperwork, get acquainted with the new manager, and prepare my workstation. I also took the time to walk around the salon and introduce myself to the rest of the staff. Having been in the beauty industry for over fifteen years, I thought I would recognize some of the people. Surprisingly, I recognized only a few from the last time I had been there. Camelot had been open almost a year. I had heard that some of the original staff had left, but I hadn't thought much about it. Not having talked to anyone who had left, I assumed that it was normal for a new business to lose staff as the working routine established itself. The salon was just as beautiful as I had remembered it; the spaciousness and attention to detail were still inviting, but something had changed.

The day I started work I overheard a conversation in the employee lounge as I was walking in. Two stylists were standing together facing the wall, making a pot of coffee, when one said to the other, "Just give her a couple of weeks, and she'll figure out that this is not what she thinks it is. She'll be sorry she came here, just like the rest of us." I turned around and walked out without being noticed. What I did notice was a huge knot forming in my stomach. I remembered seeing my mother washing clothes in her old-fashioned washer when I was a child. At times, the washer's agitation cycle knotted up the contents, causing the washer to halt. She would reach in and pull out the knotted mess and try to pry it apart. I wished she were with me at that moment to pull the knot out of me. All I could think of was that I had just escaped from the Danas dominion, I was questioning my marriage, and now I might have made a mistake coming to Camelot. The good news was that my head was now beginning to throb, and I was forgetting about the knot in my stomach.

As the weeks passed, both the head throb and the knot in my stomach increased. I learned about the cast of characters and questionable activities going on in the salon. Cammy, the gorgeous, tall, redheaded manicurist with the spectacular figure who modeled negligees from the salon at a nearby nightclub, was really a prostitute. She came for a high price—one thousand dollars for two hours, and that did not include oral sex. According to stories that she shared with others in the employee lounge, many of the women whose nails she manicured during the day were wives of the men she serviced at night. At the salon she quietly sat and filed their nails and calluses and smiled, listening to the women talk about the great family travel plans they were making or the beautiful new

66

home they had moved into. Life was good to them, and they worried about their husbands who worked late into the night.

Another character, a successful hairdresser, scheduled heavily with the "Who's Who of the rich and famous of Scottsdale and Phoenix," was a handsome, tall, well-built, forty-year-old who had just married a young, wealthy girl. Lance was also very gay. His long-time lover, although temporarily upset by the situation, understood that someday they would be together again—with children to raise. That was their plan.

The bride's mother, the most admired member of the Junior League of Phoenix, was delighted that her daughter had managed to catch one of the most handsome and popular bachelors in Phoenix. The wedding had been the event of the year. Newspapers were filled with photos of the stunning couple and their guests at a posh Phoenix resort. Everyone in the salon was talking about the event of the year and the deception of the year.

Diane, another gorgeous woman who worked as a stylist, had finally had sex-change surgery and was now on her way to being a woman at the age of forty-five. She had fathered four children and could no longer tolerate living trapped in a man's body. I liked Diane. She was bright, funny, and at six-feet-two, with long arms and big hands, she could reach anything up high in the dispensary. Diane loved her children and spoke fondly of them and their mother. I was still struggling with my own marriage and thought how simple my challenges were compared to hers, his, theirs…. whoever!

Then there was Jeff, the colorist—the despondent, broken-hearted flamer who enjoyed the pain of living. No one ever stayed with him long enough to get to know him completely. No one understood his pain, and certainly no one cared enough to hear the sickening story of his agonizing childhood and subsequent aching adult life. To put it kindly, it was exasperating to talk with him. The conversation only went one way…from bad to worse! I had heard his stories over and over until I could no longer stand to hear his high-pitched, exaggerated, whiney voice. His explicit descriptions of his sexual activities and the abuse he tolerated from his partners besieged us in the employee lounge. It became impossible to eat in the room if he was present. Even worse, he told the same stories to his clients all day long. Yuck!

I had been working at Camelot for less than two weeks when a new client appeared. David Martin was tall, dark, and handsome. His brown eyes, inviting smile, and sensual appearance could distract a group of post-menopausal women playing bingo in a casino, and believe me that *is* hard to do! David dressed in gorgeous, expensive attire. From his Italian leather shoes, Giorgio Armani suits, to the faint fragrance of something wonderful on his clean-shaven face and neck, he was a beautiful sight for hungry eyes.

David had moved to Arizona from New York. His father owned the largest chain of grocery stores in the country. David's responsibility to the father was to diversify the incredible wealth of the family business and invest in the real estate market of Arizona. He would be purchasing land and developing both residential communities and commercial centers. He had been in Scottsdale less than a month when he came in for his first haircut. He had simply walked in the front door of Camelot, and I had an available appointment. After his first haircut, David made appointments for the next six months. We scheduled Wednesday mornings at 8:30 every other week.

David was married and had two young children under the age of five. His wife had not yet moved to Scottsdale. She would stay back East until their home in Scottsdale was completed. The plan was not to sell the home in New York; instead it would be their get-away from the Arizona heat in the summer months. Not wanting to be away from his children for too long a time, David would commute every weekend until the family could make the final move in a few months.

David never refused to answer any of my questions, no matter what subject we talked about. My favorite topic was his passion for travel and adventure. Hearing him recount stories of people, places and experiences, I'd imagine what he was describing. His preferred countries were Israel and Italy, two countries in which he had attended school. His family actually owned homes in Italy and the Caribbean. As a child, he had attended boarding schools and began his international travels through educational exchange programs.

David had spent time in Switzerland, France, and Spain. For years he studied and learned the cultures of people in other countries. He was encouraged to learn several languages fluently, which he did. Occasionally, during his appointment we would converse only in Spanish, which he spoke amazingly well.

Throughout my years as a stylist, I had noticed that most successful, handsome men were usually extremely arrogant with highly-inflated egos. David's manner was just the opposite. He was calm, gentle, and considerate. He spoke of his wife and children lovingly and respectfully and talked about his parents in the same manner. He felt a great desire to give back to his parents for all that they had given to him and wanted to make a success of the new construction company that he now managed.

Regrettably, the real estate market in Arizona was a disaster, but he enjoyed the process of building. Beginning with the excavation of the land, the construction of the buildings, the plans for landscaping, and the choice of toilets (he had a thing about well-functioning toilets), he relished the entire creation. Our time together went quickly. Although I did not ask his age, I guessed him to be about ten years older than I, which would put him in his mid-forties. The conversations were always entertaining and educational. In some amusing way, he gave me hope.

The owners of Camelot were Ed and Ann Shuck, a couple in their fifties. The salon was their first undertaking in the beauty industry. They owned an offshore investment company and, according to those who knew them, were extremely successful at investing other people's money. Ed was a quiet man who said little and smiled even less. He was mostly into managing the investment company. He reminded me of a man stuck in the 1950's in the Pat Boone era. He wore white patent-leather shoes, brown polyester pants, and short-sleeved polo shirts. His hair was cut every fourteen days into a flat top with *sidewalls*. Ed was a short man in good physical shape. The smell of his Old Spice cologne always preceded him into the room.

Ann was tall and pear-shaped with large, wide hips, narrow shoulders, and a small bust. She wore inexpensive, tight clothes that emphasized her wide hips. Because of problems with her feet, she wore distasteful orthopedic shoes. Her hairstyle was a Bubble that had been out of style for almost two decades. She was unfriendly and walked through the salon with an air of distant observation. Ann tried very hard to fit into the beauty business, but if you understand the beauty industry, you know that you either fit the profile or you don't. There is a definite look of creativity and uniqueness with people who enter the beauty industry. It is an unmistakable way of addressing the world. The way they dress and that "new haircut, new make-up, new manicure will make everything better" attitude is the foundation of their worldview. Hard as they tried, Ann and her husband did not fit the profile.

In my sixth month at Camelot, all hell broke loose. The fourth salon manager, who had been with us for only two months, stormed out the door on a busy Saturday afternoon. He was yelling at Ann and calling her an idiot as he walked out. A week later, one of the receptionists left crying, claiming that she would file a suit against the owners for fraud. The receptionist was Valerie, who had taken me and my friend on our first tour of Camelot. Valerie was a capable worker and a genuinely good person. Months earlier in the employee lounge, I admitted to her that we had called her Vanna White. With the sweetest smile, she thanked me and said that she had never considered herself as beautiful as Vanna. She said, "I'll take the compliment!"

Two days after the manager quit, Ann announced that her son, Larry, would be the new manager. Like an unexpected head-on collision, chaos began as Larry took over the salon.

Many of my hair products were not being ordered, supplies were not being reordered, and the cleaning staff was fired. I was beginning to see client services deteriorate as supplies dwindled and the staff was being pushed to do more with less. The number of employees had dwindled from sixty to twenty-eight. The spaciousness and energy of the salon that had initially attracted me had been replaced by emptiness and apprehension. Those who remained, including myself, worked like hamsters running on an endless wheel, looking ahead and pretending that the most important step was the next one.

The employee lounge had become the center of rumor-mongering. Nothing was sacred in this room. No matter what was said, it was repeated and embellished before it even left the room. What I heard about the owner's son, Larry, was that he was a selfish, twenty-eight-year-old spoiled, immature brat who drank too much and had a drug problem. He had tried his hand at several careers and had failed at all of them. Married, with a young son and pregnant wife, he continued to run around town with other women while his mother spoiled him and believed all of his lies and promises. The stepfather wanted little to do with him but succumbed to his wife's wishes to keep the family peace. This was the scoop I picked up in the lounge. I had no way of knowing what was true and what was exaggerated, but none of it sounded good.

Six months passed and somehow the salon remained open. Larry spent part of his days flirting with the young, beautiful women who came in for services. He tried to manage the salon, but his inexperience in the industry was noticeable to all of us. We did not care for his casual, evasive style at handling problems. His "leave it alone and it will work itself out" approach offended the clients and infuriated the staff. Another flaw in his management style was that he played favorites with the staff. If he liked you, his hand extended out to you and he welcomed you to the top of his mountain where he felt like a king. If he didn't like you, he wouldn't bother with you. This "welcome to my kingdom if you are worthy," was anything but nurturing and supportive, which is what the staff needed most. And speaking of extending his hand to you, if you inadvertently moved too close to him, you would get one of his hands on you—always, of course, "accidentally."

Supposedly, Larry was out canvassing the city most of the day, marketing the spa to corporate clients and selling packages for a "Day at Camelot" as reward packages for employees. This was a great sales concept, but I'm not sure how much time he really spent knocking on doors. It was becoming apparent that Larry was drinking more and handling the salon less. At crucial times during the day when we needed answers to questions or decisions to be made, he was nowhere to be found. The reign of King Larry was coming to an end. He was falling off his mountain quickly, and all the king's horses and all the king's men couldn't put King Larry back together again.

A long year had passed since I had started working at Camelot. Much had changed at the salon and just as much was happening at home. My husband was struggling getting his new business off the ground. No matter how much money we put into his search and recruiting firm, the numbers were still down. It wasn't just his business; the economy in the country was headed downward. This was probably not the best time for starting a headhunting firm. Companies were letting go of hundreds of employees, and no one was going to pay a recruiting fee. There were thousands out of work who were flooding the market with their own resumes. He was forced to let go of most of the people working for him. Only two men remained. The secretary was long gone and the two who stayed were threatening to leave if business didn't pick up soon.

Within the first six months in business, we had run out of money in our savings accounts and had maxed out our charge cards. I couldn't work enough hours and make sufficient money to make up for what he needed. My commissions paid for food, cars, insurance, utilities, clothing and day-to-day expenses. For the past nine months, I had even given my husband money to make our monthly house payments. My income was the only thing keeping us going.

He wanted to use my son's college fund that I had been building for years, but I would not allow it. I knew that if we used that money, it would never be replaced.

What I feared most began to happen. During the day, he called me at the salon to see if I was busy. Believe me, I knew it wasn't my well-being he was interested in. He had begun to come home late every night. Some nights he didn't come home at all, claiming that had slept at his office and turned the phones off so he could sleep. (There were no cell phones back then). He had also started drinking again, which he had quit doing during the second year of our marriage. I sent my son to stay with his father as much as possible, and I threw myself deeper into work. Similar to the time when he locked himself into the room, I was seeing him very little, but this time he was out of the house. The months passed slowly.

One Saturday afternoon, my assistant came up to me while I was cutting someone's hair and told me that Ann wished to see me in her office as soon as possible. I thought I might be in trouble. The past weekend, on Saturday evening after work, several of us gals took a joy ride in the salon limo and drank a couple of six-packs of Corona beer. We also had some chips and salsa and leftover slices of pastrami that we found in the salon fridge. Six women, two six-packs of beer— not enough to get anyone drunk. We just had lots of fun riding around town in the back of a big limo and jumping into the salon Jacuzzi in our underwear.

Perhaps someone had seen the limo parked outside the adult toy store, which had been a stop we made. None of us had actually gone inside the store. We had only sat in the limo in the parking lot and watched people go in and come out. We had the best laugh when we recognized one of our clients, a person we would never have expected to see in a place like that. Boy, if the church ever found out what he did late at night, he might get a slap on the wrist!

As I walked into the tiny, cramped office, Ann stood up and extended her hand. "It's always good to see you, Hilda," she said as she released my hand and pointed to a chair that barely fit inside the door. The salon computer nerd, Frank, sat at the computer working with his eyes riveted to the screen. He rarely looked up from the screen or said a word to anyone. "You know Frank?" she said, pointing to him. "I do," I answered, looking over at him, wondering if he had squealed about the Saturday evening joy ride. Maybe he had been in the office when we had left in the limo. My mind was racing when Ann interrupted. "I want to talk to you about something very serious."

"Oh shit," I thought to myself, "We've been caught! This is it. She found out, and I'm getting fired."

A month before the limo ride, I had come home from work to find signed divorce papers on our kitchen counter with a note from my husband. He said that he was going to disappear from the face of the earth and I would not be able to find him again. Not only did he leave, but he had taken all of the money in my son's college fund. He had forged my signature on our joint checking account that I used to pay the monthly bills and had withdrawn the money. It was all gone. Soon after that, I received a notice that our home was being repossessed. I also found out that my husband had not filed our tax returns in five years. The debt he left behind was insurmountable. He was lucky he had disappeared—I wanted to kill him! The good news was that I was beginning to have feelings. It had been a long time since I had allowed myself to feel anything, and now I was feeling the urge to strangle him with my bare hands.

Ann continued: "My husband, Ed, and I have been talking about you for some time. You have been a solid employee at the salon for over a year. Everyone likes you, and you have a positive presence here. You are always busy, and it is obvious that the clients trust you."

"For God's sake," I thought, "just fire me and get it over with! A joy ride in the limo did not deserve all of this conversation. Now she's going to tell how I will disappoint my clients when they find out that I'm untrustworthy." I sat there with one of those fake smiles that all of us learn to give at times when we're really not sure how we are supposed to behave.

"Frank says that your numbers are consistent and that he never hears any complaints about you," she was still going on. "You know, I just don't know enough about this business to be effective. I need someone who really knows the industry and that the staff trusts and respects. Ed and I think you're the best fit for the job as our new manager."

I was still smiling, but only because my teeth were stuck to my upper lip. I think I was having an anxiety attack, which I had been having lately. I couldn't tell what I was feeling, but I was definitely uncomfortable. What could I possibly say to her? At that moment I would have preferred that she had said, "I know about the limo ride, the beer, and the Jacuzzi, and you're fired!" It would take the pressure off having to make such a big decision. Plus, I was beginning to hate working there. All I needed was an excuse to leave, but I didn't want to be the one to say, "I'm leaving!"

"Before you give us an answer, let me tell you what we are prepared to do for you financially." Money! I hadn't thought about the money, but this might be the answer to my prayers. The IRS had called the day before and wanted to meet with me to make arrangements for payments of the past five years' taxes, plus interest, plus penalties. "We are prepared to raise your current 50% commission to 60%, and we will pay you an extra twelve hundred dollars a month. We will put you into our management medical insurance plan and increase what we currently put into your 401K. Also, we will give you a bonus at the end of the year, which will be calculated on the profits that we see from your efforts with the staff."

Not my best response, but I stood up to leave the room and extended my hand to Ann. I thanked her and told her there was much for me to think about. I needed time over the weekend, and I would let her know my decision on Monday. She handed me a sheet of paper where she had written down her offer and said, "Don't feel pressured. As of today, Larry will no longer be with us. I will be taking over until we replace him. I know I can trust you not to share this conversation or information with anyone, but we do have to move quickly." As I walked out of the room, I felt myself go into a state of shock. The safety net of denial had gone out from under me. I was numb.

On the following Monday, I arrived early at the salon to find Ann sitting at the desk in her tiny office having breakfast. Frank was on the computer, also having his breakfast—a Coke. Ann, with a mouthful of muffin, motioned for me to enter. I began by saying, "Ann, I am a good hairstylist, I get along with just about anyone, and I am a very hard worker, but I don't know how to manage people. I have never done it before, and I am afraid that, under the circumstances, you need an experienced manager. I really don't think that I'm qualified to do the job. I'm scared to death that I will screw up and make matters worse."

Ann answered quickly, "I understand how you must feel. It has been difficult here since the start, but I am determined that it can work. I am aware that you have never managed before. I have called around (she looked at Frank, who had probably done the calling) and we know about you. What I know is that you are a good, solid woman." (I wondered what she would think if she knew about my crazy marriage). She continued, "I know I can trust you. I need someone I can trust to be honest with me. That's all I'm asking of you, and I know you can do that for us. I don't expect you to know everything at first, but we are committed to helping you grow into the position. If you need to take classes, we will provide it for you at our cost. I need your help now or the doors will have to close at Camelot."

Oh, damn it anyway! I came in here to say no and now I felt as if I had just had the most inspirational talk of my life. At that point it really was the most inspirational talk I had ever heard, not to mention the responsibility that I was feeling for the rest of the staff.

"And one more thing," Ann said, "I know about the limo ride, the Jacuzzi, the beer and stolen pastrami. A manager cannot be involved in those activities—it takes away trust."

The next words out of my mouth were, "I think I can do it, Ann. Be patient, and I will give you 150% of me." I heard Frank open his top desk drawer and pull out some papers. I glanced over to see a management contract. With the contract there was also a pile of flyers to be given to each staff member and placed in the employee lounge announcing my new management position. Staring at his computer, Frank never looked up at me. He just pushed the pile of papers toward Ann and continued working. Now that I thought about it, I had never heard Frank speak a word.... ever. Maybe that was a good thing. I had been right from the very first day when I looked inside the dispensary and thought that whoever organized the details of storage and labeling probably did not have a personal life. Frank's life was the salon and this computer.

The next day I began my day as the new manager of Camelot. My first objective was to familiarize myself with every person and each department in which they worked. From the reception desk, barbershop, boutique and spa areas to the upstairs manicurists, skin care and stylists, I wanted to hear what they had to say about working there.

I started with Jill. She was one of my favorite employees, who single-handedly managed the reception desk. She was bright, respectful toward clients, and incredibly efficient. Although she kept to herself and did not get involved in the employees' lounge gossip, she knew everything that was going on in the salon. During my meeting with her, she cautioned me that something was going on that wasn't quite ethical. She wasn't sure, but she suspected that someone was stealing money. I knew Jill would not make such an accusation if she did not have something on which to base this information. She felt uneasy and thought that she was being lied to by the owners.

To my surprise, all the other staff that I talked with felt the same. Their biggest concern was the employee 401K programs. Having already had the terrible experience with Mr. Danas and his 401K thefts, I understood their hesitancy, but, as manager of Camelot, I was required to participate by investing $5,000 up front into the plan. Because I did not have the money, it would be taken out of my paycheck over the next few months. Hesitant as I was, I felt that as the manager, in good faith, I had to show my trust and confidence in the owners.

Eventually, I met with everyone and talked about their goals in the beauty industry and how Camelot could best support their goals. Several quit when I took over management, saying that I was not qualified, which was true, so I hired new stylists, manicurists and a masseuse. Frank remained in the downstairs department, and I hired a new cleaning person. Most of the staff who had been there when I started had left. Before long, the attitude in the salon began to be more positive.

In my desire to have the staff get to know Ann better, I talked to her about being friendlier toward them. With the Christmas holidays on the way, I suggested a company party. Ann agreed to have it at their home. She also asked if I would take her shopping for new clothes, and would I change her hairdo? I was delighted that we were communicating.

Meantime, my client, David Martin, continued to be a wealth of information and a great inspiration. When I shared with him that I had taken over the management position for Camelot, he was excited for my new opportunity. We discussed strategies for planning and implementing new systems that would provide structure and quality control for the staff. We talked about different management styles and how to develop better communication skills. We also discussed ways to improve support systems that would better sustain and nurture the existing staff. David gave me some great advice about the employee lounge, suggesting that I hang positive posters and inspirational quotes around the room. His thought was that as the staff felt better about management and became busier making more money, gossip in the lounge would stop. He was right. The staff had made changes for the better. It was obvious not only to the employees but to the clients, who commented that their visits had become more pleasurable.

On a Wednesday morning, during his appointment, David asked if I would like to see some of the projects that he was working on. I was delighted that he asked, and we set a time for the next Monday. We would meet at the salon and he would do the driving. When I arrived the next Monday at our scheduled time, he was waiting for me in the lobby.

I had a wonderful time talking with David and seeing several office buildings, a shopping center, and a subdivision of homes he was developing. He also drove me past his home that was just days from being completed. He appeared excited as he talked about his family moving to Scottsdale.

After our drive around town, we stopped for lunch at a small restaurant in downtown Scottsdale. Soup and salad and a great discussion gave me hope that, someday, I too, would have an honest and good man in my life. It was an unforgettable day.

A month later, David asked if he could bring in his family for me to cut their hair. I welcomed the opportunity to meet them. Andrew, five, and Alexis, three, were absolutely gorgeous children. Not only were they physically beautiful with dark, curly hair, and big, round, sparkling eyes, but their manners were polite and their social skills were sophisticated.

David's wife, Rachael, was a dazzling woman of medium height. She was slender with long, dark hair, olive skin, and big, round eyes the color of black olives like the children's. She was dressed impeccably, and her jewelry was impressive. They were a dramatic couple. How fortunate I felt to have met her and how happy I felt for David that he had created such a good family. I also felt closer to him after meeting his family. We had become good friends.

One year after I began my management position, I became physically and emotionally ill. My hours had been long and intense. On-the-job management training, continuing to carry a full clientele of over five hundred, supervising a staff of thirty, and going through a divorce had caught up with me. Struggling with anxiety and a debilitating eating disorder, and weighing only ninety pounds, I asked if I could step down from my management duties. I suggested a capable woman, Cathy, as my replacement. I had hired her as a stylist six months earlier. She had managed the previous salon in which she worked, and I knew her to be well-qualified, optimistic, and talented. What a gift she was for me and the salon! Ann agreed to let Cathy to take over if I would stay on as a stylist. The staff welcomed Cathy whole-heartedly.

Six months later, I received a phone call from Cathy early on a Sunday morning. She said that she had to talk to me immediately. It was imperative that we meet in person and not talk on the phone. I asked her to come right over to the apartment where I was now living. To my surprise, Carl, one of the other stylists I had also hired, was with her.

We sat in the living room and Carl began: "I received a phone call last night from someone who will remain anonymous. This person would lose their job if they were identified and would possibly go to jail for doing what they have done. This person gave me information about the owners of our salon. The federal government is investigating Ann and Ed. It seems as if we are working for very dishonest people. They are suspected of stealing money, not only from our 401K's but also from all of the clients invested in their offshore investment company. We are talking millions of dollars here. This is a serious crime."

"What can happen to us in the salon?" I asked.

"The word is that our salon is under surveillance and that the phones are being tapped. Because Ann spends so much time there, they are listening to all the conversations. Every one of us is being scrutinized because we could be part of their cover-up. The feds are not disregarding anyone. The caller said that Ed and Ann are dangerous."

The three of us sat silently staring at each other. We drew a deep breath simultaneously.

"There is more," he continued. "The feds are going to take over the salon and lock the doors during the investigation. That means that all our tools and client files—everything we use to make a living—will be locked up and held in the building for an indefinite length of time. We need to get out now!"

Every stylist who worked at Camelot had signed a non-compete contract for three years. If the employee left before the contract ended, the hairstylist had to pay Camelot $3,000. Not only did the money have to be paid to release the contract, the stylist was not allowed to work within a five-mile radius of Camelot. I had re-signed a contract when I began my management position two years earlier. Cathy and Carl had contracts that were less than a year old.

We sat in the living room of my apartment and made a plan. I would resign my position as a stylist. My first task would be to find a salon owner who would be willing to hire me, pay off my contract, and possibly hire several others. Chances were that when I left, Ann would call it quits. I was the only one left from the original group who was bringing in a substantial amount of money. She had said that I would be her last manager, and even though she had allowed Cathy to take over my position, I knew Ann hoped that someday I would be well enough to take the position again.

Cathy, Carl and I agreed that we would never discuss our conversation with anyone. We might jeopardize others in the salon and, if Ann and Ed were doing something illegal, we did not want to stand in the way of the feds stopping them. As Carl and Cathy stood at the door, I joked, "With the way our luck has been running at Camelot, Ed and Ann might be some of America's most wanted criminals. Wouldn't that be something?"

For several hours, I sat and thought about my life at Camelot. I felt a huge responsibility for those I had hired and would now be leaving behind, although Carl and Cathy assured me that they would deal with it. My only hope was that after I left, the salon would close its doors and everyone would be released from their contracts before the feds took over.

Two days later, I walked into a salon just one mile away from Camelot and talked to the owner, William, whom I had met briefly at a hair show. Without going into detail, I asked him if he would like to hire me and possibly six other staff from a competitive salon. The hook was that I needed him to pay off my contract. Within an hour, we came to an agreement. He would pay off the contract. I could start as soon as I could set up my station, and I would bring my assistant, Jill, who had been the receptionist at Camelot.

Giving notice to Cathy was much easier than having to tell Ann that I was leaving. William had given me a check to give Camelot in exchange for canceling the contract. Cathy waited for me to take my tools, equipment, and client files out of the salon before calling Ann to notify her that I had left. Cathy assured me that she would do everything she could to get my 401K information to me as soon as possible. At this point I had well over $10,000 invested in the program—a lot of money to me!

That evening Cathy called to inform me that the salon had closed. Camelot was finished. When Cathy called Ann at her downtown investment office to let her know that I was gone, Ann had rushed over to the salon. She sat with Cathy and Frank (who was still there working on the computer), and after a thirty-minute conversation, the decision was made to close the salon.

The next morning, Cathy, Carl, and four other stylists joined me at the new salon. We were relieved to settle in where we could be together. Now we could relax and concentrate on our clients and put the experience of Camelot behind us.

Ann and her husband had been good to me, but as the investigation went on, I was finding out who they really were. Millions of dollars had indeed been stolen from the investors and from all of us at Camelot. None of us who had invested in our 401K's would ever see the money again. It was gone to some bank account in another country. I remembered Ann saying to me on the day that she offered me the management position, "I need someone that I can trust and who will do the *honest* thing. That's all I'm asking of you, and I know you can do that for us." I, in turn, had entrusted myself to them and expected that they would do the honest thing for me. All the rumors and accusations regarding Ann and Ed were true. They had been lying to all of us.

Months later, while I was watching television with a friend, I saw Ann and Ed's faces appear on the screen. They were fugitives wanted by the authorities. Underneath their photo it read, "America's most wanted. Dangerous."

My friend David Martin followed me to the new salon. He established his bi-monthly appointments on the salon master book, and we settled into our usual routine— Wednesday morning at 8:30, every other week.

The new salon was not the spacious, luxurious place that we had come from, but it provided us a space where we could all be together. Some clients followed us and some didn't. At least we were settled for now.

Three months passed very quickly. We were entering the holiday season again, the busiest time of the year in the beauty industry. Everyone wants to look their best during this time of festivities and winter visitors. We were jamming at the salon, working longer hours and harder days. David had just left the salon when the receptionist announced over the intercom that I had a phone call. Usually, the receptionist made all our appointments, so the only phone calls we took were personal. It was David on the phone. He asked if I would meet him for lunch the following Monday as he had a business proposal for me. I accepted and didn't think about it again.

The following Monday morning as I dressed for the day, I began to think about what David might want to offer me. I had seen a beautiful shopping center that he had built. I wondered if he might want to have a great salon as a tenant. We had known each other for three years now. He knew he could rely on me. I was dependable, trustworthy, loyal and committed to the profession. I would have to work on my management skills or maybe Cathy would come along and manage the salon. I would co-own the salon with David. The others from Camelot would also come with us. We would have a gorgeous salon again—David would see to it.

My mind ran away with me as I thought of all the possibilities of working for and with David. His wife and children could come in for haircuts anytime they wanted. And speaking of his wife and children, I had not seen them since the one time they had come in and that was at least a year ago. There had been so much going on that I had not asked him about them. I felt so selfish. I would have to apologize to him as soon as I met him for lunch.

I walked into the lobby of the Hyatt at Gainey Ranch, where he had asked me to meet him. It is one of my favorite resorts in Scottsdale. Walking down the stairs into the restaurant, I could hardly contain myself. The idea of David offering me a salon had now become bigger than life in my mind. "Mr. Martin," I said to the hostess. "Yes, this way please, and watch your step." There were two more steps down to the main floor. I wondered if she could tell that my legs were shaking. I felt like a newborn fawn trying to stand with long, spindly sticks for legs and big feet attached at the bottom. Awkwardly, I followed the hostess to the back of the room where I could see David waiting for me.

As he saw us walking toward him, he stood to pull out my chair. I appreciated his gentlemanly manners. Having my chair pulled out for me to be seated always made me feel special.

I consciously took a deep breath and asked my legs to settle down and relax. I still thought David Martin was one of the most attractive men that I had ever met. He was wearing a beautiful dark grey, pinstriped suit with a white shirt and a fabulous red tie. On his shirt pocket were his embroidered initials. I had never paid that much attention to the initials of the monogram before. They spelled out DAM, David Andrew Martin. Damn, I thought, how did I miss that before?

He made small talk for a moment and then said, "I really need to talk to you about something very important, and I can't wait any longer."

"Of course," I said. "I'm here to listen."

He began, "I've given this a lot of thought. This is not

something that has come easily to me. I've spent time assessing my life and your life also. I hope you don't think I am trying to control you in any way by what I am about to ask of you. It's only that I know what I want, and I am hopeful that you will understand my question."

He took a deep breath and stared at me with his beautiful, piercing eyes and continued. "We have known each other for three years. I have spent time getting to know you, not only as my hairstylist, but also as a high-quality woman. I know that you have been through a lot in your personal life with your former husband, and I am truly sorry that you have had to struggle so much."

"How did you find out about my former husband?" I asked.

"That doesn't matter. I have ways of finding out anything. But I must continue. I will always be married to my wife Rachael. She is the mother of my children. Our parents planned our marriage. It was the way it had to be. We have known each other since we were children. Our parents are life-long friends and business partners. There was no other choice but to marry each other. She is a good woman, and I have a special love for her. We will never divorce."

"Why are you telling me all this?" I asked. "I thought you were going to make me a business proposition."

"I am," he said. "But first I want you to know this information, and now I want you to have this."

From underneath the table, he picked up a gift box, a medium-sized, shiny white box with a large red ribbon tied into a floppy bow. He handed it to me across the table. I pushed my chair back a bit and placed the box on my lap to open it. As I untied the ribbon, I began to shake all over. I still did not understand what this was about, and I was getting nervous. The ribbon came off easily, and I lifted the box cover. As I opened the tissue paper, I pulled out a gorgeous, emerald green, silk teddy—the kind you sleep in at night, or at least go to bed wearing.

We sat quietly for what seemed like a very long time. I gently folded the teddy and put it back into the box and left it on my lap. He broke the silence. "I'd like you to consider being my mistress."

My mouth could not form words. I was stunned as I sat there not knowing what to do or say. He continued, "My wife has left to go back to New York, and she will not be coming back. She does not like Arizona. She misses her family, and the children miss their grandparents. We came to Arizona for several reasons. One of them was to see if we could fall in love with each other. It isn't working for either of us. We do not have that kind of love for each other."

My mind raced to what seemed like a million times that I had been with him before. It would never be the same again. This moment had changed our relationship forever. "David, do I look like a whore to you?" I asked across the table with a low voice.

"Absolutely not," he said quickly. "I'm not looking for a whore to spend time with. That's why I am asking *you.*" There was silence again. Then he proceeded, "As I said at the beginning, I have given this a lot of thought. This is not easy for me to ask of you, but I want you in my life. I'm being very honest with you. The connections I have with my wife are our children and our parents. We both agree that a divorce is not an option at this time, and maybe never, but neither of us wants to live together. Our parents do not know about any of this, nor do we want to tell them anything until the children are older.

"I want you to be with me. We will travel together. I will live in Scottsdale, and Rachael will live in New York. I will go back to see the children and bring them out here as much as possible. I cannot promise you anything other than my love and respect for you. I have fallen in love with you over the past three years. And this is all I can give you right now. Maybe mistress is not the correct term to use for what I am offering you. The question is, will you consider being with me?"

As if I had stepped into a vacuum, the restaurant disappeared around me. The look on David's face etched into that place in my mind where unforgettable faces are stored. I observed myself stand, gather my belongings, including the gift box, and make my way to the stairs. I don't recall if I heard his voice behind me. Walking up the stairs, legs numb, not feeling my feet touch the steps, like a caged zoo animal being led back into its den for the evening's rest, I felt prodded by something that I could not identify. I wanted to leave; yet I wanted to stay. I had been excited and nervous for an opportunity that would change my life, but I had not expected anything like this! I wanted to stay. What if this was the opportunity of a lifetime?

Days turned into weeks and weeks into months. I missed seeing David every fourteen days. I missed our conversations. I missed seeing the world through his vivid descriptions of places he had visited and lived in. I missed being inspired by his ideas, and I missed his input on business dealings and transactions, but, mostly, I missed being with him. Only once did I hear from him after that Monday lunch. One year later, he called me from New York on a Wednesday morning at 8:30 and asked if I would consider having dinner with him that evening while he was in Scottsdale on business. I answered, "No."

Snip-It

Jan was in the salon today for her double weave, haircut, and blow dry. She walked in obviously upset. By the look on her face, the posture of her body, and the way she carried her purse, it was clear that she was upset with her husband. Women know that kind of stuff.

As soon as she sat in my chair she began: "He can never find anything around the house. No matter where I am or what I'm doing, he'll yell, 'Jan, have you seen the such and such? I don't know where you put my things. I can never find anything around here!'

"When we were first married and he started doing that, it drove me nuts. Now, thirty-four years later, it really makes me angry. We have discussed this over and over again but nothing changes. He still thinks that I purposely hide things from him."

Jan and I have had this discussion many times, and I can tell that she is losing patience with him.

Before I can drape her or throw a towel around her neck, she continues telling me how upset she is. Looking up at me with her beautiful big, blue eyes, with a sigh of desperation and a serious tone to her voice, she says, "I don't understand it, Hilda. He thinks that my uterus is a finding device."

Portrait Of A Family

Every thirty minutes another personality walks in the door with a unique story. No two people are alike, and yet each person has similarities that connect them in our salon. How incredible life is with its human parallels of survival, needs, and desires and its cultural, religious, and political differences!

This Thursday morning the sun comes up while we are already at work. It is November, the beginning of our busiest time of year. Our phone is ringing off the hook, which is music to my ears because the ringing gives me a sense of job security. When you're in business for yourself, the last thing you want is a silent phone.

Michelle and I are the only ones working in the salon. Thank God for Michelle. She has been my loyal and trusted assistant for the past seven years. Our relationship reminds me of the characters Radar O'Reilly and Colonel Blake in the television series *M-A-S-H*. Every thought that Blake has is superseded by Radar's quick, intuitive mind. There is nothing that Blake can think, want, or do without Radar knowing ahead of time. Just like Blake and Radar, as I begin to ask Michelle a question, she will either answer it or hand me the thing I was going to ask for before I can finish asking. Fortunately for me, Michelle has only the best intentions toward me, or she could be dangerous.

Dr. Wise is on the phone with news that his wife's mother passed away yesterday. They are both leaving for New York this afternoon for the memorial service. I have promised him some of my *Conscious Eating* books for the next time he gives a group presentation. (Several years ago I wrote and published a small book of meal blessings. I still have hundreds of them in my garage, and I give them away gladly to whoever wants them. In the salon I have been known to perform a variety of unofficial services: counselor, dietician, medical doctor, and psychic.)

Dr. Wise, a psychologist, lectures around the country. His focus is on the challenges of weight control and the benefits of a spiritual attitude toward weight loss. Because he and his wife are leaving and will not return until the morning of his presentation, he asks if he can come by *now* and pick up the twenty books I have promised. As I begin to say, "Let me have Michelle go downstairs to my car and see if I have twenty books in the trunk," I see that she is already halfway down the hall heading toward the front door, and she has my car keys. Promising that we will call him back in a few minutes, I hang up and continue working on my client.

There are two clients in the salon at this early hour and a third is expected in about ten minutes. Hopefully, she will be on time today. Her track record isn't the best. She's on our "worst-lies-for-being-late" list. The rest of our day is booked with another sixteen clients, and we cannot afford for anyone to walk in the door late. Each and every client is as excited to see us as we are to see him or her. After all, a hair appointment is not like going to the dentist for a root canal or to the hospital for a colonoscopy. Hair appointments are pleasant and rewarding.

Sitting in my chair is my client, Esther, whose thirteen-year-old daughter, Chloe, has confessed to giving blowjobs to the boys at school. The daughter doesn't see anything wrong with what she's doing. Her best girlfriend is doing it too. She says it isn't like having sex: "It's only a blowjob. Even President Clinton said it isn't sex," she says. Esther is despondent and doesn't know who to talk to at this point. I happen to be the first adult, other than her husband (who doesn't count), that she has talked to since last night's conversation with her daughter. Her husband, who did not want to have this child to begin with, will blame Esther for not paying closer attention to her teenage activities.

Chloe is the youngest of their five children, and Esther doesn't remember having challenges like this with their other children when they were the same age. Maybe it's because she

90

and her husband are now in their fifties, and they are simply tired. Or just maybe they have become a bit lax about curfews and follow-up calls to other parents, making sure that the teenagers are where they say they are going to be. Who knows? The other four children have complained that Chloe has gotten away with murder since the day she was born. Maybe they're right!

Nonetheless, the most dreadful part of this mess for Esther is that her daughter could think that giving a blowjob is actually something fun to do! At this point in our conversation, Esther admits to me that she has never given a blowjob, nor would her husband ever expect her to. "Thank God for small favors," Esther says in a quiet, relieved voice.

In the second chair, off to my right, is my client, Peg, who is getting over a flu bug. Her skin is still pasty white and her energy level is low. Perhaps a little touch-up color with a bit more red and a shorter cut and style will make her feel better, although the real problem is the fact that her son is struggling with depression and refuses to get help. Her son is a handsome young man, twenty-one years old and a senior at the University of California. The last time she and her husband drove to visit him, they found him living in squalor, alone, and emaciated from not eating. Apparently, the young man is brilliant and doing well academically but not doing well socially or physically. Not wanting to admit that he might be in trouble psychologically, Peg is worried sick. He will not shower, brush his teeth, do his laundry or clean his apartment. He refuses to eat anything except for an occasional pizza that he has delivered and the rest of the time he drinks diet Coke. "He's beginning to look like an escapee from a POW camp," she says with a voice of a worried mother.

This is not the first time that I have heard this story from a parent. During the years, especially the more recent years, clients have shared similar stories with me about their children. I don't have an answer to this dilemma. My only thought is that it must be a sign of the times. As a young woman in my early twenties, my mother would have not allowed me to behave that way. Back then there were hard consequences, scolding, and those terrible talks about disappointing and shaming the family. *Bastante*!

I think her son would benefit from medication, but I'm not going to say a word. My only responsibility to Peg today is her hair and listening. And frankly, that is all *she* wants from me!

Fortunately, Peg is a very bright woman with good psychological tools to work with. As a registered nurse in a local hospital, she will find help and support for her son and for their family while they go through this crisis. After color has been applied to her re-growth, I give her some hot tea. She has brought a novel to read, and I assure her that if she needs anything else, I am close by. Our salon is very small, so I am very close to her and everyone else in the salon at all times. Peg will wait until her timer goes off before either Michelle or I get back to her and give her some well-deserved attention.

Walking in the door, carrying twenty books for Dr. Wise, Michelle picks up the phone on the second ring. (I don't know how she does it, but somehow her timing is pretty close to perfect.) Mrs. McBride, who has been a client for twenty years and has a standing weekly appointment on Thursdays at 10:30 a.m., is on the phone asking for directions to the salon. She has been coming to us at this particular location for twelve years, every week. As far as we know she has always driven herself to the salon. We are a bit concerned that at seventy-five, she might be getting forgetful.

Mrs. McBride is a charming woman. Her love for the Arizona desert, devotion to her charismatic husband, and profound affection for her loyal ridgeback puppy warms our hearts every time she walks in the door. She is one of our most cherished clients. We can only hope that she will drive another twenty years to the salon, but on this day, that prospect isn't looking so good!

Michelle, still on the phone with her, very patiently gives her directions and reminds her to drive slowly and not to rush. Considering Mrs. McBride's appointment is not for another hour and a half and it only takes her fifteen minutes to drive to the salon, we feel sure that she will be on time.

After talking with Mrs. McBride, Michelle calls Dr. Wise to let him know that the books will be ready when he arrives. He wants to know if there is a possibility of squeezing him in for a haircut. I get that look from Michelle that is frustration and rescuer all rolled into one pathetic stare, as she says, "Dr. Wise forgot to make an appointment the last time he was in. Can we accommodate him?"

"Does anyone ever take any responsibility for their own lives?" I say very quietly so as not to be heard by anyone but Michelle. "Why does his lack of planning become our problem?" (Sometimes I get into a self-important posture and think that my time is the most important thing in the entire universe—I hate it when I do that—but I'm doing it at that very moment.)

Michelle very gently says into the phone, "We don't think we can squeeze you in today, Dr. Wise. We'll see you when you pick up the books, and I'll make you an appointment for next week. Please accept our condolences for your lovely wife and the rest of the family."

Now I'm feeling guilty about those attacks of self-importance. I can always spot that attitude in others, and I get so judgmental and feel sooooo offended by *those people*, but when I'm doing it, it's somehow different. I can sooooo justify it!

My schedule in the salon resembles a succession of dominos, perfectly lined up one after another. The first client of the day begins the sequence. It would be wonderful if all clients understood their personal responsibility of showing up on time. Similar to *one* domino falling out of order and causing an upset to the entire arrangement, when a client shows up late, our day becomes a series of hurry up and catch up, hurry up and catch up. One late client can disrupt our entire day.

If you think I might be a little anal about being on time or that I might be exaggerating, I would have to agree with you. Managing my schedule with a sense of order and staying

93

on time has become an obsession throughout the thirty years that I have been working as a stylist. I have allowed the mania of running on time to somehow define me and determine whether people respect me or not. Try as I might, I cannot change my thinking about this.

Perhaps, all these years, I have been in the wrong profession. Maybe I should have been a bartender instead where the time you show up isn't an issue. I would see customers on a regular basis and they could show up at whatever time they felt like coming in. They would tell me their story and I would listen. Reaching across the bar, I could gently pat their hand and tell them how sorry I was to hear their story. Giving them another drink, similar to dispensing medication, I would feel as if I had done something wonderful for them.

I have obsessed over this time issue forever, and I don't get anywhere. It always stays the same. I am still a hairdresser trying desperately to run my daily schedule and run it on time. It's like men thinking they know exactly what women are thinking...all the time. Is that ridiculous, or what! (Sometimes I wish I had never quit drinking. This would be a great time for a cold beer, a glass of white wine, or even a margarita with salt on the rim of the glass. Actually, any alcohol would do.)

Back to my obsession with time. I know, without a shadow of doubt, that as a bartender, I would eventually begin to expect the regular customers to show up at a customary time. And if they were not there, I would begin to take it personally. Feeling disrespected, I would begin to worry about *my* schedule and put myself in the same place where I am right now! Needless to say, the "on time" fixation is not about the clients, it is about me. *What... me controlling?*

Why don't I just fire the clients who continually come in late? I have and I do. However, some are too entertaining to let go, and others I still hold some hope for. How many times can I sit face to face with a client and ask, "What can I do to help you come in on time except for that silly-ass game of scheduling your appointment thirty minutes later than your real appointment and telling you that your appointment is thirty minutes earlier, which I refuse to play?" Usually, the client apologizes and promises to be on time "from now on." This lasts for about two appointments.

Actually, all this late stuff is just part of a game we play. Michelle and I have a rating system of who can tell the best lie about being late. Although lately when the client runs in the door as if crossing the finish line of a twenty-six-mile marathon, breathlessly giving us a fabulous new excuse, more often than not we don't even listen to the explanation. We just get moving faster into the "hurry up and catch up, hurry up and catch up" mode.

Peg's timer has gone off and our third client, Martha, has walked in the door sixteen minutes late. "Oh…the traffic was just terrible on Shea Boulevard. I can't believe how terrible people drive! People are such idiots. Doesn't anyone pay any attention to the speed limit around here? Those Snowbirds are back in town for the season and are driving like Arizona desert turtles. They make my life a living hell," Martha is being *the traffic victim*. She continues, looking around to see if anyone is listening to her complaining, "You wouldn't believe how much I tried to be on time." (No, we wouldn't believe it today or any other day, Michelle and I are thinking without looking at each other for confirmation. We just keep working.)

"We're glad you made it today, Martha. Have a seat and we'll be right with you," I say as I begin to cut Peg's hair.

Martha grabs a magazine and looks around to see if she sees any familiar faces. She wants someone to talk to, but since no one is making eye contact with her, she sits quietly waiting her turn.

We actually like Martha as a client. Her sense of humor and her ability to tell a captivating story keep the clients entertained. Her area of expertise and where she creates the most interesting storyline is in dysfunctional family matters. Martha's family is endowed with a gamut of characters, unusual events, and a never-ending array of fanatical behavior.

Occasionally, even the neighbors get included in the chaos. I'm sure that if you were to look up the word *dysfunctional* in Webster's Dictionary, you would most likely find a photo of Martha with her family and her friends—all smiling happily.

An eighty-five-year-old live-in mother–in-law, a drug-addicted, bi-polar step-son who shows up every few months when he runs out of money, and five other children from Martha's previous marriages have supplied enough entertainment to keep her name firmly in our appointment book. Did I forget to mention that Martha also has three brothers and four sisters whose lives are as colorful as hers?

Of course, some days we have more time than others to enjoy her comedic story about the family saga or the next door neighbor who is "out of his freaking mind!" Today we will move her along as quickly as possible, or as Michelle would say, "Slam her down, suds her up, blow her out, take her money, and send her packing!"

In the beginning, I had that "please be on time" conversation with Martha until I began to sound like one of those mothers who nags her child endlessly with the warning, "If you do that again, I will have to punish you," which is followed by doing nothing when the child does the very thing he was asked not to do. The child hears the mother's voice like a scratch on a music CD…stuck and repeating.

Every time we had the "talk," Martha would give me that glazed-eyed, silly smile with her head held to appear to be paying attention and then—nothing! All the same, this client is worth keeping around. Until I decide to either retire or disappear from the face of the earth, Martha will be on our preferred always-late client list.

Making eye contact with Michelle, I ask her to prepare a "cocktail" for Martha: Urgent Repair with a touch of Pure-Tech, bag her, give her high heat for 10 minutes, cool for 5 and rinse with cold water.

For those of you who are unfamiliar with salon "cocktails," they are not an alcoholic drink with a floating umbrella stuck in a wedge of lime. A hair cocktail is a treatment made up of an assortment of conditioners, sealers, strengtheners, and possibly color rejuvenators that are applied to a client's clean, wet hair for deep conditioning and restoration of faded hair color. Ideally, we lightly condition every time a client comes in for any service. A "cocktail" is applied when the client's hair arrives DOA (Dead on Arrival) or when we need catch-up time, as in Martha's case. Since she's late for her appointment, we are now into the next client, who has arrived very early. We must stall Martha until there is an opening to squeeze her back into the schedule. The good news is that her hair will benefit. Martha has the best-conditioned head of hair in our salon. Hurry up and catch up, hurry up and catch up, hurry up and catch up!

It is now two in the afternoon. Everyone with a morning appointment has come and gone, including our sweet Mrs. McBride who came in an hour early and patiently waited. She says she doesn't mind waiting. I think she must find it entertaining to sit and watch the goings-on. It's like watching a play. A new character is introduced to the story every half hour or so and brings the ability to change the entire mood of the scene. It actually feels that way to me at times. I honestly don't know how the day will develop and end until it's over. There are so many variables that influence the ending. That's what keeps it interesting and entertaining. I love working in my salon. Just like the production of a play, I can have a proposed script for the day, set the stage, and give everyone *their* scripts, but the real drama unfolds with each character and how they perform.

Esther left feeling better about her daughter's blowjob announcement and has decided to call the mother of Chloe's best friend. Together they will tackle the situation and take the next step in getting help for the girls. "The good news," she said as she was leaving, "is that the girls are not having intercourse with those boys." As I watch Esther walk out the door, I think to myself…. "Not yet!"

Peg has a new hairstyle and is feeling better. Dr. Wise has picked up the books and made an appointment for the end of next week for his haircut and color. After a refreshing "cocktail," haircut and blow dry, we have sent Martha packing to her next appointment.

The next client arrives. Krista is a terrific gal. She is in her mid-fifties, single, brunette, (about a level 5 color, if you're a hairstylist reading this) with a sweet and welcoming personality. Her big, brown eyes are soft, her smile is quick and gentle, and it's obvious by her temperament that she is a gentle soul. Krista has been a client just short of two years. I see her every five weeks for a cut and style and occasionally a body wave. At her first appointment we connected quickly with each other, not only because she has great hair to work with, but also because she is a marvelous storyteller and a budding writer.

On this day she begins to tell me the story of one of her siblings who has recently gotten in trouble with the police. Recalling the birth of her baby brother, Krista talks about his coming home from the hospital. Everything appeared normal. He had hands, feet, and a head. He cried, ate and pooped. He had a penis and testicles just like all other boys. However, as a young teenager, he was sent to an institution because he would not behave like a boy and insisted on dressing like a girl. The institution, punishment, and ridicule only made matters worse, and at the age of fourteen, he left home to discover who and what he was.

Krista had some disturbing news about her brother, who presently calls himself Stella and lives in Seattle. She explained that Stella, who is now forty years old, has always worked the system. Most recently "she" has stolen her older brother's identity. The first thing she did with the false identity was to rent an apartment. In the files the manager wrote, "She presents herself as a woman but uses a man's driver's license." However, in Seattle, laws prevent the manager from questioning this. Stella had also gotten credit cards in her brother's name. The brother had impeccable credit, but now his credit scores have dropped significantly. The interesting part is that no one wants to use past police reports because they say it is a victimless crime or a white-collar crime. It takes the brother days to get someone to listen to him. When Stella is finally arrested, they discover that she is also suspected as being part of an auto theft ring in her apartment complex. They think she is alerting the thieves when someone isn't home or if a "good" car is available in the parking lot.

Krista continues to explain that Stella has been involved in criminal behavior for quite some time. She does whatever she has to do to support herself and has no remorse for her behavior. The catch is that when they do arrest her, there is no place to hold her in jail. (This probably means she has not had a surgical sex change.) The police have told her brother that she has a list of arrests for drugs and other crimes. The problem is not having enough to arrest her on, but where to put her.

As I listen to Krista telling her story, I realize that I have not thought about what happens to transsexuals who have not had had surgery. Are they treated like a man or a woman? Who makes the final decision? And most importantly, will they ever feel safe, accepted, and happy? Concerned, I think to myself, there is still so much that I don't know.

Our next client, Dianna, walks in the door. Dianna is one of our preferred clients. Once in a while, she is a few minutes late for her appointment, but we enjoy her so much that we rarely notice. (Hard to believe, isn't it?) She is a bi-monthly client. Her long, thick, multicolored blonde hair requires lots of attention. It's expensive and time-consuming to be a stunning "natural" blonde. The process of keeping a beautiful blonde head of hair presentable is a full-time job for the one wearing it. The paybacks of spending hours in the salon are great-looking hair, lots of attention, and those blonde jokes that everyone is sick and tired of hearing.

Dianna is not only a stunning woman on the outside—tall, slender, perfect facial features, blue eyes, full lips—she is also beautiful on the inside. We have never had a moment of discomfort or disagreement with her. I say this because several weeks ago I made a mistake and applied the wrong color to her gorgeous hair. I accidentally mixed a darker color (*much* darker) and applied it to her re-growth. Because we were very busy and she sat out in the waiting area, I did not see her until her timer went off thirty minutes later and she walked back into the salon. It was almost black! "No problem," Dianna said when she saw herself in the mirror. "It will fade within days. Don't worry about it, Hilda. It'll be just fine." Now that is a great client! This is also a good place to note that Dianna is so beautiful that if she were wearing a floor mop on her head, she would still look great. Furthermore, in thirty-odd years of hairdressing, this is only the second time that I have mixed the wrong color for a client. Honest!

On this day, with the correct color on her hair, Dianna makes herself a cup of instant coffee (the kind that looks like tea bags, which she keeps a supply of at our salon) and chooses to sit in the lobby to read a magazine. Thank goodness for little blessings during a busy day....clients who require little entertainment.

Molly Stride, a seventeen-year-old with naturally white-blonde hair, big blue eyes, and the sweetest smile in the whole world, walks in the door. I have been her hairstylist from the beginning of her life, and I am tickled to see her. I have a special relationship with this young woman, and, as she walks in and we hug each other hello, I hold back my tears. Molly's life is about to change dramatically...again.

It was eighteen years ago that I received the phone call. It was a busy day with clients stacked up all around me. A friend called from Ohio to let me know that she was five months pregnant, and would I know of a couple in Scottsdale who would like to adopt the baby? I knew two couples who would jump at the chance. Either couple would be wonderful parents. Financially they could give a baby every opportunity in which to grow and flourish.

Taking a few moments to gather my thoughts, I told my friend that as soon as I finished wrapping a perm and got some of my clients moved out, I would call the couples and see who I reached reach first.

My friend from Ohio was a bright, loving woman in her early twenties who had been dating the same young man for three years. They had decided to get married, but as the date approached, she changed her mind. She did not feel ready to be married. And she was pregnant.

After catching up with my clients, I called the first couple, but no one answered. On the first ring of the second phone call, my client, Marissa, answered.

"Hi, Marissa, it's me, your favorite hairdresser," I said, teasing her.

"Hi, favorite hairdresser, what can I do for you?" Marissa asked in a cheerful voice.

"Marissa, I have a baby for you and your husband. Are you still interested in adopting?"

"Oh, my God, Hilda! Yes! Let me give you the number of our attorney."

That was almost eighteen years ago. Marissa and her husband had brought Molly home from the hospital the day after she was born and adopted her.

During the years, I had wondered if and when Molly would want to meet her biological mother and if I would be given the opportunity to help. That time had come.

Two weeks earlier, I had received a phone call from Molly's mother. "It's time, Hilda. Molly wants to meet her biological mother. She will be eighteen in a month, and she says she's ready."

After several phone calls, I reconnected with my friend, who was no longer living in Ohio, and whom I had not talked to in years. She was thrilled to hear that Molly wanted to meet her and happily agreed. I passed this information along to Marissa and plans were coming together for a meeting between the families. (Did I forget to add "baby broker" to the list of unofficial services that I offer?)

Dianna's hair color has turned out gorgeous. She is happy and we are thrilled with the million-dollar look that she gets every two weeks. By the time she is ninety, she will most likely have spent close to a million dollars on her hair. Oh well…such is the price we pay for beauty. I'm just happy it's me on the receiving end of the million dollars.

One more day at the salon has ended. On the drive home, I have the idea of sending a greeting card to each client who came in that day. I shall send Dr. Wise a thank you card for distributing my books at his lectures, along with a sympathy card for his wife. For Esther I shall choose one of those "You Are a Terrific Mother" cards with the sweet flowers and encouraging words, cheering her on, to keep on keeping-on. Peg will receive a card reminding her that she also is a great mom and that this situation too shall be diagnosed, treated, and eventually will pass. Like all stages of life, we deal with them and ideally learn and grow in the process.

Mrs. McBride will enjoy a greeting card featuring a puppy. I will let her know how much I appreciate her being our client. Enclosed will be a map to the salon.

Martha's card will encourage her to keep trying to come in on time. Included in the card will be a rabbit's foot to hang on her rear-view mirror or, better yet, a Saint Christopher medal that she can attach to her dashboard (Does anyone use those anymore? Or did they do away with that saint also?) Krista's card will simply say "Great Stories, Keep Writing."

For Dianna, I will send her a gratitude card for once again reminding me, simply by her presence, that beautiful and uncomplicated women still exist! No matter what challenges are happening around her, she handles everything in a calm, responsive manner…always expecting the best. And guess what? The best always comes to her…. picture that!

I will send a special card to Molly and her mother thanking them for letting me be part of their lives, although words cannot describe what I feel as I think of Molly and the joy she has brought to her adoptive parents.

As for the rest of the day's clients, a "thank you" note of acknowledgement will do. I honestly appreciate every person who walks in the door. Each one brings a different personality to our salon family, just as brothers and sisters do. We have our "ultra-responsible firstborns" like Esther and Peg, the "left-out middle-children" like Krista, the "spoiled babies" like Martha, who follow no rules and are appalled by anyone who tries to set boundaries for them, and we have the wise elders of the family, like Mrs. McBride—precious ones who, in the winter of their life journey, begin to chill out and forget unimportant things, like directions to their favorite places.

Our salon has plenty of dysfunction to keep it interesting, but most importantly, we have an incredible support system within this family of individuals who, by outward appearance, don't fit together. As I ponder this, I recall that just like a family, we all came together in a recent crisis that changed my assistant Michelle's life forever.

It was the Friday before the Memorial Day holiday, and Michelle and I were finishing up a very busy week. We had one client in the shampoo chair, one client still coming in, and we were in our tenth hour of working. We were both dog tired!

As Michelle began to shampoo the client who had been waiting, her cell phone rang. This was unusual because her phone rarely rings at the salon. I asked her if she needed to answer it. As a mother, I know that it is important to answer all calls, especially since Michelle has an eleven-year-old son. She told me that whoever it was could leave a message and she would call them later. No sooner had it stopped ringing when it began to ring again. "Hmmm..." I thought. "Michelle, I'll take over. It must be important."

One of the attributes that I appreciate about Michelle is her attention to our clients. As I walked toward the shampoo area, her cell phone rang for the third time. This time I insisted: "Go, Michelle. It's okay. I'll finish this. It could be about your son or your husband." The *mom* tone of my voice left no room for argument.

Michelle stepped outside and walked down the hallway to answer the call. Listening to my client with one ear and trying to listen to Michelle with the other, I began to get concerned when all I heard was a repetition of shaky "Okays," and then, "Where do I need to go?" As she thanked the caller and finished the call, I glanced up in the mirror and saw her walk through the door. As long as I live, I will never forget the look on her face. The color had gone form her normally rosy cheeks, her eyes held a look of shock, and her lips were trembling.

By this time the client was sitting in my chair, and I had begun the styling process. I put down my blow dryer and asked Michelle what had happened.

She replied in a shaky voice, "That was the commander from the Air Force. My husband stopped breathing during his training flight on an F-16, and they did CPR on him for fifty minutes. He's in critical condition, and they don't know if he will make it through the night. I have to get to Florida tonight. I have to call his parents. I have to pick up my son. I have to call my parents. I have to get a ticket and fly to Miami, Florida tonight. I have to...."

I stopped her there and said, "Okay, sweetheart, one thing at a time. Let's slow down." As I said this, I put my arms around her, telling her to take a deep breath with me. All that existed in that moment was our breath, the client momentarily forgotten.

Michelle had met her husband when she was sixteen. They had dated for five years and then married. Four years later, they'd had a son. Like any marriage, they'd had their ups and downs but had worked through them. Just a few months ago, they had celebrated their fifteenth anniversary and her husband's fortieth birthday.

Although I hadn't known them in the beginning of their relationship, Michelle was fond of telling me that it was because of working in the salon that she and her husband were still together and that the last five years had been the best years of their marriage.

When Michelle and I first met, I was working on my doctorate. I asked her to participate in my research sessions in counseling as a case study. As I counseled her and got to know her, I enjoyed her sweet, giving nature and thought that my clients would appreciate and enjoy her. After counseling her for a year, I released her from my research and asked her to come and work with me at the salon. She had been an elementary school teacher for ten years and had no experience in a beauty salon, but I assured her that I would train her.

She agreed to my offer and began working part-time for the first year and full-time afterwards. That had been seven years ago.

Working in the salon and having the advantage of being with a diverse group of clients, Michelle began to understand the importance of self-discovery, self-acceptance and self-defense. The self-defense aspect is an important part of learning to set boundaries and speaking up for oneself. Believe me, in a hair salon, one has to learn this rule to survive!

Some of our clients are brilliant, educated leaders in our community. They are involved in the social, economical, technical, political, spiritual and medical industries throughout our city. Others are great mothers, resourceful homemakers, loyal wives, devoted volunteers, and sensitive people who care deeply about life. All of these clients embraced Michelle like a daughter or sister or good friend and made her feel welcome from her first day.

The connections that Michelle made with these caring people, along with the growth that her husband experienced in joining the Air Force Reserves, helped them bond as a couple and a family like they never had before. He had been her first, her one and only love, and in that moment after the phone call she didn't know what she would do without him.

The first phone call Michelle made was to her husband's parents, who live in Tucson, just an hour and a half away from Scottsdale. They were not home. She left a message for them to call her immediately on her cell. Quickly, she made her second call to the airlines from our salon phone, leaving her cell open. It was the holiday weekend and there was not one flight available that evening. Her cell phone rang, and this time it was the commander calling. He was trying to get flights out for her and her son also and was not having any luck either.

Meantime I had begun my own phone calling. I called my next client and asked if we could reschedule his appointment due to an emergency. Then, remembering my client still in my chair, I quickly finished her hair and sent her out of the salon. I don't recall if we charged her for her hair that day. We, including the client, were in that numb, safe place that the mind and body go when dealing with a crisis. All we could do was what was right in front of us. The rest of it would line up and get taken care of as needed.

It suddenly occurred to Michelle that she could call her in-laws on their cell phone. When they answered the call, she tried to keep herself composed as she explained what she knew. Two months earlier, Michelle's husband had been in Iraq. His parents' greatest fear during that time was that they would receive a call that something had happened to their only son. Michelle's biggest fear had been having to make that call. He had come home safely, but now this had happened.

The next challenge was how to get all of them to Florida as soon as possible. We were both in shock, and we couldn't think of what to do. Looking at each other, we stood motionless, waiting for something. What next?

Suddenly I thought of Judy, a client who is a travel agent. I grabbed my cell phone and called her. She answered immediately. As I explained the situation to her, she gasped and said, "Oh my God, is Michelle okay? Tell her not to worry, I will find a flight for her and her son and her in-laws."

Miracle upon miracle, Judy was able to secure four seats on a sold-out flight at no charge. Considering the holiday weekend, this was no easy feat! To this day, we have no idea how she accomplished this. All we know is that she and America West somehow made it happen.

Everything catapulted into fast motion. Michelle and I closed the salon and walked quickly down the hallway holding hands. We had an unspoken agreement that we were going to be together during this time. Making sure that she was okay to drive, I sent her home to pack their bags. I picked up Michelle's son from his after-school program and called a client who owns a dog-sitting service. She agreed to take care of the family dog.

As Michelle raced home to pack, all the while answering the phone for updates on her husband's condition, she tried to calm herself. She does not remember the drive home.

Within twenty minutes, I arrived at their home with her son. She was walking around the living room in circles, upset that they were out of dog food. I knew that we had to re-center her. This was a monumental situation, and there was no getting around it. It was vital that she pull herself together.

"Michelle, do you want to tell your son what is going on? I have not told him anything."

As if a light had gone on in her head, she immediately responded and said, "Hey, Buddy, your dad is in the hospital in Florida, and we have to go there tonight. Go upstairs and pack your suitcase because we have to leave as soon as possible." I could tell by the tone of her voice that she was back on track.

Assuring Michelle that I had called the dog sitter and that I would pick up dog food and get the house keys to her, we could now move on to the next task at hand. I ran upstairs and finished packing Michelle's suitcase with the clothes that she had thrown on the bed while she answered the phone calls. Her son packed his bag and dragged it down the stairs. I recall him asking, "Mom, what games should I bring to play with Dad?"

We drove to the airport quietly. Her son did not understand the gravity of the situation, and there was no use in making things more difficult for either of them. When we arrived, I hugged them goodbye, asking her to call me as soon as she knew anything. I reminded her that whatever happened, I was here for her. She thanked me for everything and disappeared through the doors, already carrying the weight of the world on her shoulders.

I went home and began calling my clients. Not knowing when Michelle would be back at work, I needed to reschedule them. Without an assistant, it's impossible for me to handle heavily scheduled days. As I began the phone calls and shared with clients what was happening, prayer chains were activated in every religion imaginable—Christian, Jewish, Buddhist, New Thought, and Baha'i, to name a few. Like a spreading Arizona wild fire, clients volunteered to call others they knew from the salon. Some knew each other before coming to the salon and others had become friendly with each other during their monthly appointments.

For the next two days, Michelle and I stayed in touch. If she didn't call me within a few hours, I called her. The diagnosis was grim. She wanted a miracle, and I wanted to give it to her, but, in the end, the thing that we knew was inevitable happened. Her husband passed away. She was now a widow at the tender age of thirty-six, and her son was now without a father. Her in-laws had lost their only son. My heart ached for her and the rest of the family. I now had the sad task of telling the clients.

Word spread quickly about Michelle's loss. In the next couple of weeks, the outpouring of love and support that came from our clients was something that most people only see in those touching Hallmark movies. The clients, this unlikely family, wrapped Michelle and her son in a blanket of cards, phone calls, emails, and monetary gifts. When all was said and done, she had received hundreds of cards and thousands of dollars. The generosity of the clients astonished me, and, because of them, Michelle did not have to worry where she would get the funds to pay for the memorial service, to house visiting family, and support her son and herself while she grieved her loss. This deluge of support reminded me how good people are. In spite of what we hear in the media where so much that is reported is bad, I know that people are naturally good and want to help others.

Clients continue to give her moral and spiritual support. Each time I hear one of them ask Michelle how she is, how her son is doing, and if there is anything she needs, I am reminded that the beauty salon is not just about the business of doing hair but about building relationships. Some relationships extend through a lifetime; others last for just one appointment. But always there are the tendrils of the web that inexplicably draw us together as one.

We may not always agree on our thoughts about religion, or how we vote politically, or what we eat or wear, or what constitutes good mental health, but in our salon, great relationships are first, and the desire for beauty is what brings us together.

I am finally arriving home after a long day at the salon. As I turn into my driveway, I think I just might be too tired tonight to send out those greeting cards...perhaps another day.

Snip-It

No matter how much I try to keep up with fashion trends, hair styles and the latest in what women are doing to themselves to look their best, I can't seem to stay ahead of the race.

Today's conversation among the ladies in the salon was about elective cosmetic surgery. I'm familiar with facelifts, nose jobs, ear tucks, and eyelid lifts. I'm not as familiar with Botox and other boosters for smoothing out wrinkles and filling in where Mother Nature is "failing." Of course, let us not forget that boobs, butts, arms, tummies, and thighs are still everyone's favorite body parts to have pumped, lifted up, or suctioned out. Don't even get me started on tattooing and body piercing! Someday people will wake up, look at themselves in the mirror and say, "What was I thinking?"

Which reminds me. Several months ago I attended a conference in Carmel, California. It was a spiritual gathering with hundreds of participants. One woman, who was at least ninety years old, caught my attention. I saw her often during the workshops and larger gatherings and could not stop staring at her. Considering her age, she wore very skimpy clothing, which I found unusual. Typically, as we age, we tend to cover up our maturing bodies. It was difficult to ignore her skimpy attire and even more difficult to disregard the fact that she was covered with tattoos.

Now let me tell you, a body that has aged to that degree and is covered with faded ink, is *not* a pretty sight. When the skin begins to melt downward, it *all* goes down. Her worn-out tattoos reminded me of Salvador Dali's famous painting, "Soft Watch at the Moment of First Explosion." Time is melting down and *s t r e t c h i n g*. I'm sure she was a lovely lady and I commend her for her spirit of adventure, but it was hard to look past the choices of her past…they were written all over her body.

Nevertheless, I thought I had seen and heard it all until a delightful group of women in the salon, all from a nearby synagogue, began talking about the newest craze in cosmetic surgery: the Aussie Makeover—a labia lift for the most delicate parts "down under."

I couldn't believe my ears. For those women who shave down under, the labia lift is a definite must. You certainly don't want that poor, helpless part of your worn-out body hanging on you. What if someone were to see you out somewhere and say, "Did you notice her floppy labia? Can you believe that she goes out looking like that? What is she thinking?"

Another client who had been through chemotherapy for breast cancer and had lost all of her hair...everywhere.... chimed in and said that in her opinion, "Some things are better left alone and hairy!" I think she was talking about her labia after four children and years of married life with a wild and sexually demanding man. (I should be jealous.)

Honest to God, I had never laughed as hard as I did that day with those women. We talked about organizing a panty raid, having a show-and-tell party and naming our labias just like men name their penises.

The discussion had just about run its course when my next client walked in the door. Tom is married with two grown daughters. He's easy-going and has a fun spirit. He asked as he walked in, "I could hear all of you laughing the minute I stepped in the front door. What's so funny?"

111

Hair Balls and Angels

In my years of listening and observing, I've noticed that people who enjoy deliberately hurting others, demanding unnecessary attention, and complaining about everything are nothing more than frightened, unhappy children. The word "children" refers to adults who have not matured and developed the characteristics of responsible grown-ups. Once these frightened, unhappy children are firmly placed in your life as family members or as coworkers in a job you otherwise love, or as clients you can't get rid of because they are connected to more desirable clients, they can become a learning experience in teaching you how to speak up, set boundaries, become conscious of what is *really* important to you, or simply how to become more accepting. As if you needed another learning experience!

I affectionately call these clients *Hair Balls*, which I use to describe not only the problem cats have from licking their fur, but also the problems I have when these clients get stuck in my life. Dealing with them makes my throat clog up the way it does when I get the skins of too many almonds stuck in my throat. We serve almonds in the salon, and I munch on them during the day. But when I put too many of them in my mouth, they remain tightly positioned in my throat, neither coming up nor going down. These little cloggers frustrate me to the very end of my nerves, and yet I forget from one handful of almonds to the next how to eat them correctly—that is, slowing down and paying attention. It has been this same rushing, inattentive pattern that has caused me to end up with *Hair Ball* clients. Red flags scream at me, "She's going to be difficult! Don't take her on as a client! Stop! She will NEVER be happy!"

One such *Hair Ball* was a woman I picked up during a "Getting Rid of Fear Forever" workshop, which we both attended. We spent two months attending the weekly, three-hour workshop in which we were given information about the natural process of fear and how to benefit from it instead of being paralyzed by it. One of the most important principles we were taught was that fear is an indicator for measuring one's growth. If people are spending too much time in their comfort zone and not feeling afraid about anything, they might not be growing and stretching themselves enough. In other words, fear is a necessary emotion for human development.

Each class built on the class from the week before, and one could actually measure the clutch of fear decreasing as the weeks passed. The instructor, a woman who had suffered with anxiety and panic disorder, was well-versed on the subject and was passionate about helping others better understand their fears. She was well-informed, interesting and had created a variety of exercises and homework assignments to help anchor the new information for the participants.

Over the course of the two months, working closely and sharing intimate stories about our fears, several of us in class had a bonding experience of sorts. We exchanged phone numbers and email addresses and promised to keep in touch. One of the participants, Bella, took a special liking to me in the first class and attached herself to me like Velcro on a pair of tennis shoes. Two weeks after the workshop ended, Bella came to the salon for her first hair appointment.

Bella was married and had three children. She and her husband had transferred from New York to Arizona twelve years earlier when they decided to stop fighting the winters and shoveling the snow. Her husband worked for an office furniture warehouse while Bella stayed home to raise the children. Nervous by nature and with lots of excess energy, Bella spent most of her time talking on the phone, shopping, and decorating their new home in Scottsdale.

During the weeks that we spent in the fear class, Bella was quiet and reserved as she participated in the group exercises and overall class involvement. The large group, over eighty participants, made it easy for her to remain unnoticed.

One story Bella did share in a small group was the fear that she had around her mother, who was an extremely controlling, demanding, wealthy widow. Apparently, Bella's mother bought her love by the amount of money she gave Bella. Having become accustomed to the monthly checks, Bella's biggest fear was that her mother would become angry and stop funding the family's lifestyle. There was a continual fight between Bella and her mother, which, in turn, affected Bella's relationship with her husband and the children. Fortunately, Bella's mother lived in New York. Unfortunately, she came to visit often, and they talked on the phone several times a day.

Although Bella appeared to be kind and gracious during our weeks together in the fear class, in the salon her true character came to life. As if she had a completely separate personality from the one I had met in class, in my chair she was antagonistic and argumentative. No matter what I said, I was incorrect. And not only was I incorrect, she couldn't understand how I could possibly think that way!

Bella would then give me the "real facts" about the subject and, of course, I was wrong. Over and over again, no matter the discussion, an argument would develop. The worst part of the experience was that I would actually get caught up in the disagreement and argue back. I hate arguing, but it was obvious that disagreement was sport for Bella, one that she had perfected with her mother.

As a client, she developed a pattern that went something like this: Bella would arrive very early for her appointment, at times as much as an hour early. She would sit in the waiting area just outside the door and look through magazines as if she were angry at the contents. Like a child throwing a tantrum, she turned each piece of paper forcefully, using her entire body to express her distaste for each page. She then made sounds of disgust and frustration to go along with her disapproval. *Agh! Oh! Disgusting! Please!* She waited impatiently, getting up occasionally to peek into the studio to see if we might be ready for her. Feeling no pressure, of course, I'd smile and assure her that we would be on time. I came to know that Bella's life motto was that the world was a dangerous place to live in and that before anyone could hurt her, she was going to hurt them! She fought to control life around her continually, even to the point of trying to control the time of her hair appointments.

Once in my chair, Bella would complain about the last forty years of terrible haircuts, weaves, and hairdressers who simply did not understand her hair. I stood behind her and listened intently to every word. Relaying the information back to her to make sure I understood her instructions as best I could, I began working on her hair. Moving slowly through each section and talking to her about my reason for doing it a certain way, taking her lead on the size of the brush to use for the blow dry, I did the very best I could. When I thought I was finished, I would stand back and ask her if she liked it!

Sulking, she would appear as if she were about to cry and then she would say that she was sorry for being so difficult. Then, on to the best part of the drama. Aggressively, she would begin pulling at her hair—brushing and pulling at it as if a family of black widows had colonized in her thick, curly, bleached hair, and she was frantically trying to yank them out.

During one appointment, in the brushing and pulling frenzy, Bella grabbed the blow dryer from my hand and yelled at me that I didn't even know how to blow-dry correctly. Then she started yelling at her mother as if she were standing next to her. As if someone had screamed, "FIRE!" the salon emptied out. Clients went to the restroom, got coffee from the hall vending machine, or stepped outdoors to check on the beautiful Arizona weather. It didn't matter that the temperature was one hundred and twenty degrees outside. It was better than staying in the room with Bella and her invisible mother.

I know what you're thinking. You're thinking that I'm making this up, but I'm not. This woman needed help, more than a good hair day could give her. And as much as I tried to be patient with her, there was no stopping her and there was no getting rid of her.

There were times when I thought to myself, what am I doing trying to please this woman who is clearly mentally ill?

After all, just because I took a class with her doesn't mean I'm in a committed relationship. Maybe I was trying to prove to myself that I had embodied the principles of the "Getting Rid of Fear Forever" workshop that professed that every person in our life is mirroring something in us that we must work on and transform, or the other principle that spending too much time in our comfort zone means that we are not growing enough. No matter the reason, this *Hair Ball* was stuck in my beauty salon esophagus for now.

When I suggested that another hairstylist might better understand her hair requirements, Bella would break down in tears and beg me not to throw her out of my life. She was always sorry and would promise to never cause a scene in the salon again. I would then feel really sorry for her, spray her hair, and send her out the door. And that is how our relationship continued for several months.

In contrast, Bella's husband, who also became a client, was a cheerful, nice-looking, bright, easygoing guy. He spoke well of his wife and their children. He chuckled as he acknowledged that they were an eccentric but devoted family. He did confess that he traveled much of the time and, therefore, didn't spend too much time at home with them. This might have been the reason they were still married after twenty-two years.

To hear Bella talk about her children, they were annoyances. The seventeen-year-old daughter was on constant heartburn medication for a nervous stomach. She ate only frozen foods. No fresh fruits or vegetables for her. Their smell and texture bothered her, and she thought they were creepy. Eating only twice a day because it upset her stomach, she instead drank a six-pack of soda every day and spent a lot of time in the bathroom after each of her meals. *Hmmm...*

The fourteen-year-old son was a genius. His incredible ability to understand and handle computers was uncanny. No matter the problem, he knew how to find it, fix it, and re-program it within moments. He was even capable of taking a computer completely apart, which he had done at the age of twelve, and putting it back together again. His problem was that he was already one hundred pounds overweight. He also had a little problem with stealing. A bit of a kleptomaniac, he had been in trouble with the stores at the mall and in their neighborhood.

Because she hated cooking, Bella made sure the family lived within walking distance to a grocery store. The children had the responsibility of taking care of their own meals. The fourteen-year-old, who had been forbidden to set foot in the grocery store by the manager, paid his younger brother to shop for him, which gave him more time to sit in front of the computer.

The youngest of the three children was a slight, shy, ten-year-old boy. Other than his small size, he seemed normal until you made an effort to have a conversation with him. He had a horrible speech impediment. An outsider would find it difficult to understand him, but the family had managed to compensate for his inability to communicate by ignoring him. It was obvious that this little one needed professional help. All three of the children needed therapy, but neither Bella nor her husband paid enough attention to get them help.

If you are wondering how I found out so much about the family, I actually spent time at their home with them. Bella had a way of manipulating people to do what she wanted. She had suggested that we spend some personal time together outside the salon so we could get to know each other better. After all, we had spent time bonding at the fear class. By getting to know her better, I would understand her lifestyle so that I could better understand her hair needs. The truth is that her husband traveled most of the time, she did not like spending time with her children, and she didn't have a group of women with whom to have fun. Okay, so she was lonely, and I felt sorry for her. There you have it! We met at the mall, spent half a day shopping, and then went to her home for dinner (we had take-out).

At another appointment, while I was cutting her hair, Bella mentioned that she had met and befriended the world-famous author, lecturer, scientist and authority on integrating psychology with spirituality, Lina Ann Vida. I had read every book that Ms. Vida had ever written, and I was excited for Bella and at the thought of meeting her myself. I wondered if this friendship would mellow Bella out a bit and possibly give her a picture of what a strong and successful woman was like, without the fighting feature. I assumed that Ms. Vida was like her books—thoughtful, inspiring and connected. Their relationship might change Bella's attitude for the better, and, quite possibly, all of us who knew Bella, including her husband and children, could benefit from it. It gave me hope for her life and for my sanity if she were to continue as my client.

From the beginning, Ms. Vida and Bella "immediately felt the connection of old souls meeting again," as Bella told me. It was quite a feather in her hat to name-drop such a famous world figure in the salon. "Lina Ann and I are spending lots of time together at her home in Fountain Springs. She is recovering from a stroke and enjoys my company. I go by daily and check on things for her. She really likes me," Bella said loudly while others tried not to listen.

Bella had actually appeared happy and calm that day, and, for the very first time *ever,* she liked her hair.... As if the heavens opened up and an angelic choir began singing praises from God himself, the salon was filled with a feeling of magic! She liked her hair!. The relationship with Lina Ann was already having an effect. This was a miracle.

On her next visit to the salon, I was bold enough to ask Bella if she thought that Ms. Vida would consider a visit from me. After all, I had been a fan of hers for years and had read every book that she had written. During a communications class in college, I had become interested in the subject of psychology and spirituality and the communication skills required to discuss it with others on a professional level. I had found her books remarkably helpful and intellectually stimulating. Meeting Lina Ann Vida would be the thrill of a lifetime.

Recently, I'd read that Oprah had been to Arizona to meet Ms. Vida. If it was good enough for Oprah, it was good enough for me. At the same time, I felt as though I deserved something good coming back from Bella after all the emotional turmoil she had put me through. This could be the saving grace that would keep Bella on my books. And, if the last appointment was any indication of Bella's new attitude adjustment, things were about to get better.

A week passed as I waited for Bella to call me with an answer. I am not known for my patience, so after not hearing anything, I called her.

Bella said that she was sorry that she had not called me sooner. She continued, "I talked to Lina Ann about your visit, and she said that you could come by. I will take you with me next Monday. She doesn't like people knowing where she lives, so I will drive and I will have to blindfold you until we get to her house. I think that you also need to know that Lina Ann will decide how long you will be with her. She is very direct and honest. If she does not like you, she will tell you so, and she will ask you to leave immediately. You will then leave and wait outside the back door, which I will show you when we get there. You will stand and wait for me until she excuses me. And—one more thing—she loves expensive, rich, imported chocolate. Lastly, no fragrances, no noisy jewelry, and no loud clothing."

She continued, "If she likes you, she will point to a chair, the same one that Oprah sat in, and you will sit and wait until she speaks to you. Do not under any circumstance talk to her before she talks to you. When she is ready for you to leave, she will let you know and you will get up and leave without asking any questions. Do you understand what I am telling you?"

Feeling rather uncomfortable, I said "Yes" and agreed to meet her the next Monday at her home for the drive out to Fountain Springs. All those restrictions were making me anxious already. What was I thinking to agree to such a ridiculous plan? Okay, it's just another experience, I thought to myself. I can do anything once.

Monday came quickly. After being careful not to wear anything with fragrances, anything too bright in my clothing, or anything that made any noise, like dangling earrings or charm bracelets, I was blindfolded, put in the car, and we were on our way. We were both quiet on the drive out.

It was actually rather pleasant not having her complaining about something or somebody. Thoughts were running through my mind about Ms. Vida and the questions that I wanted to ask her....only, of course, if she gave me permission. There was so much that I wanted to know about her life journey. I hoped that she was in a good mood and relaxed so that we could chat about stuff. Maybe we could become girlfriends, or at the least, I could become her new hairstylist. How wonderful would that be?

The drive to Fountain Springs took thirty-five minutes. I was almost out of my body with excitement when Bella opened the car door and walked me to a back door behind the house.

When she took my blindfold off, I was surprised by the condition of the yard, and I was even more surprised by the state the house was in. No one had taken the time to maintain either. I understood that Ms. Vida had been ill, but did she not have help? A woman as popular as she was, with all her books, appearances on television and radio, and her international lectures...I was confused by the appearance of her house.

My next thought was that the terrible condition of the house was intentional. She was obviously concerned with her safety and wanted to remain anonymous. Why else would she have Bella blindfold me? I am sure that she didn't want to be bothered by curious, adoring fans wanting to get a peek at her, like me. In spite of everything, I decided that the inside of her home had to be fabulous.

Bella finally came to take me in. We entered through the kitchen door that led through the dining room and into the family room. As we made our way through the different rooms, I noticed piles of clutter, including mail, books, dead potted plants, baskets, African masks and other unrecognizable stuff on counter tops, tables, sideboards and shelves. I was even more confused. The inside of the house had the same neglected appearance as the outside. There was mess everywhere, including piles on the floor. It was unbelievable that one person could have so much clutter, most of it junk.

As we approached the family room, I could see that the room had been turned into a hospital-like environment complete with a large hospital bed that occupied the center of the room. On either side of the bed were tables with more books, pitchers of water, boxes of chocolates, and writing material. (Oh, damn, I had forgotten her box of expensive chocolates)! A television was mounted on the wall in front of the bed for easy viewing. The remote control was attached to the bed railing.

Ms. Vida lay in bed looking straight ahead at the blaring television with her fingers on the remote control as Bella led me to the chair (the one that Oprah had sat in, I thought). I sat down quickly, hoping that she would not ask me to stand up and leave. Bella then went around the bed to the other side and sat in a chair that faced me and waited.

We sat in our chairs quietly for what seemed to be forever while Ms. Vida channel surfed. She never looked over to acknowledge me, nor did she say a word to Bella. Like two faithful, well-trained dogs, we sat and waited for our command.

Ms. Vida continued her fixation with the remote control. Over and over again, she went through the channels, only stopping for a few moments to make grunting and groaning sounds. She turned the sound louder then set the control on mute. With the mute on, she went once again around the entire selection of channels. Then she started over without the mute. The sound was very loud and uncomfortable.

Finally, after twenty minutes of not speaking to either of us, she put the television on mute. Without looking at me, she asked what kind of Indian I was. Moving forward in my chair, thrilled that she was speaking to me and had not asked me to leave yet, I answered with a nervous voice, "I am Yaqui and Mayan Indian. My father's parents, who were born in Mexico, were Indian."

She grunted and said nothing else.

We sat for another ten minutes as she continued to channel surf. Then, with a commanding tone, Ms. Vida pointed to her portable toilet chair at the foot of her bed and asked me to bring it to her. I moved quickly and obediently. I picked it up, carried it to the side of her bed, and placed it in front of the chair where I had been sitting. Bella came around to help her off the bed and asked me to wait in the adjoining room on the other side of the wall.

That room, the living room, was at least twice as cluttered as the others. Maybe because most people rarely went into the living room, nothing appeared to have been moved in years. No matter. I stood still and tried to relax. I didn't realize how uptight I was. I felt as if I had been on a death march. "How could this be?" I thought to myself. Every book that I had read that was written by Ms. Vida had been so psychologically informative. She had known so much about people and relationships. Could it be that the stroke had damaged her brain? Of course, this wasn't the same woman who had written such spiritual and loving books. This was her after her illness—afraid and unhappy. Like a fearful child, she had reverted back to feeling vulnerable. I had to adjust my attitude and appreciate this time with her. I took a deep breath.

Standing still, trying to calm myself, I tried to listen to anything that was being said on the other side of the wall. I didn't want to miss my cue to come back, if, in fact, I was going to be asked to come back. We had been there for a grueling thirty minutes. I wondered if Bella also got the silent treatment when she came by on a regular basis. I could not believe that she could tolerate this kind of treatment. As a matter of fact, instead of adjusting my attitude and calming down, I was feeling myself getting upset again.

Bella called out suddenly. "You can come back now, Hilda!"

Ms. Vida was back in her bed grasping the remote, and Bella had taken her place in her chair on the other side of the bed. The toilet had been left in front of the chair where I was sitting, so I asked Ms. Vida if I could move it. The answer was an emphatic "No."

Although the lid was down, the contents of the toilet stunk. Along with the normal discharge of human fluids, her urine had an assortment of medication that gave it an overwhelming pungent smell. And, although we can stand our own smells, most of us don't tolerate the smell of another person's urine easily, at least I don't, and especially right under my nose.

That was it for me! I had had enough. I was ready to leave. I interrupted Ms. Vida as she continued her channel surfing and asked her if there was anything that we could talk about. Without looking at me and keeping her eyes on the blaring television, she answered, "Not unless you can tell me when I'm going to feel better."

I answered back, "I guess I don't know the answer to that. Only you know."

Feeling terribly disrespectful for what I said, I sat back and waited to be admonished. I looked across at Bella. I could see by the look on her face that she was disappointed with me.

Ms. Vida's next question was odd. She asked me if I could see a color around her. I closed my eyes and immediately a color came in and replaced the black behind my eyes.

"Orange," I said out loud.

"And what does that mean?" she asked.

I sat quietly and closed my eyes again as a rush of thoughts from books and conversations with my friend, Cheryl, filled my mind. She is an expert on color therapy and the effect that color has on people.

"I seem to remember learning that orange is the color of transformation. It's not the most soothing color," I said almost apologetically.

"I hate that color!" she said quickly, still watching the television.

There was a long pause as she switched the television to mute. There was only silence. I sat debating whether to get up and leave or wait for my dismissal.

Ms. Vida reached across her bed and picked up a small guest book that was on the table in front of Bella and threw it at me. It landed on my chest first before I could get my hands on it. "Here, sign this. I like all of my guests to sign in."

I picked up a pen that was on the table next to me and prayed that the right words would come to me. I had no clue what to write. I was exhausted, and now perplexed, by our color conversation. The smell of the urine was making me sick to my stomach.

Taking a deep breath, I watched as my hand wrote the words.... *Ms. Vida, I can only wish for you that you never feel as uncomfortable as I feel at this moment. May you be well. Thank you for your time. Respectfully, Hilda Villaverde.*

Putting the pen back in its place, I stood up, placed the guest book on the chair, and thanked Ms. Vida for allowing me to spend time with her.

I looked across at Bella and told her that I would wait outside for her at the back door. Assuring her that I knew my way out and that she did not have to hurry, I turned around and walked out.

I waited outside in the depressed, hungry, thirsty yard for about ten minutes. I was angry with myself for what seem to be a million reasons. I wished that I had never met Ms. Vida and instead had kept my hero image of her intact.

Bella came out and interrupted my thoughts. "Well," she said, "that was the longest time that anyone has been with her. She must have liked you."

"I couldn't tell," I answered.

"Well, she's hard to read, but, believe me, that was absolutely the longest time that anyone has ever been with her. I know that for a fact," Bella insisted. I was sure that Oprah had been there longer, but I was not going to argue with her.

Thanking her for taking the time and for making all of the arrangements for the day, I allowed Bella to blindfold me

125

again. In my excitement to meet Ms. Vida, I had forgotten to buy the chocolates that I had planned on taking to her. I asked Bella if we could stop at the store so that she could help me choose the best chocolates. Since Bella visited her on a regular basis, she could take them with her on her next visit. We stopped and she selected some fabulous Swiss chocolates, along with a "Thank You" card that she thought was appropriate.

Bella did not bring up the fact that I had excused myself instead of waiting to be dismissed, nor did she mention whether Ms. Vida had said anything about my quick answer about her getting well, the color orange, or what I had written in her guest book. Oh, well, I would simply forget the experience. Put it out of my mind. Case closed!

Of course, I thought about it the rest of the day, week, even two weeks, morning and night. I'm an emotional, sensitive, Latina woman. Everything affects me as if I had carried it in my belly for nine years and then given birth to it. I should have been more patient with the situation. I knew Ms. Vida was still healing from her stroke, and I pushed my way in. I was afraid that I had hurt her by my note in her guest book, and she certainly didn't deserve to be treated that way, although the thought of smelling the urine right under my nose made me angry again. Mostly, my concern was that Bella would make a scene at the salon if she decided that I needed a reprimand. There was so much to think about that I forgot that fear is wonderful for personal growth. The only thing growing in me was my fear.

Wondering how I was going to fare with Bella on her next appointment was uppermost on my mind. This new, kinder, quieter Bella was not going to last much longer, especially if she kept hanging around Ms. Channel Surfing Vida.

The next two weeks stretched out as I worried myself sick about Bella's next appointment. This one was for a haircut, double weave and blow-dry—a lot of time to spend with her. I wished it were just a cut, but noooooo, it had to be one of the longest appointments.

An hour before Bella was due, my assistant announced a phone call from her. Bella let me know that she would not be coming in. She asked that I cancel all her appointments. I did not understand her, nor did she think I cared enough about her hair. Furthermore, she asked me to cancel her husband's appointments. "Hilda, you just don't get my hair, my family, or my friends! You obviously don't care enough to make an effort to know us better. And as far as your blow-dry goes, you simply aren't good at it. So BLOW DRY THIS! I'm not coming back! Ever!"

With that said, Bella hung up the phone.

As I always say… "And there you have it!"

Two years later, through a mutual acquaintance, I heard that Bella and her husband had divorced and that she was dating a wonderful man, a few years younger than she, who had never been married. Her husband was navigating the Internet dating services and was having a great time with lots of different women. Bella's mother had passed away from a sudden heart attack, and Bella was in court fighting with her brother over the inheritance. The mother had left most of the money to Bella's brother and some money to Bella's children, but the children could not touch a penny until they reached the age of twenty-one. Bella did not get anything.

As for Ms. Vida, a year after my unforgettable visit, I saw her at a bookstore in a wheel chair accompanied by a genteel looking woman who I assumed was her care giver. I wondered if she was feeling stronger and less afraid. I hoped so for her sake. She had been such a vital woman and had touched so many in such a positive way.

I noticed that Ms. Vida's hair was a mess. I could have done something really wonderful with that head of hair, I thought to myself. I felt the irritation of almond skins clogging my throat as I walked past her and smiled at her. She did not smile back. Instead, she looked away.

At the beginning of this story, I said that most adults who behave badly are frightened, unhappy children who never grow up to take responsibility for their actions. Bella's story is about a child who had been deeply wounded and consequently developed behaviors to survive in her environment. Her life ripples like a stone that is thrown in the still water of a lake. Each current is felt by those around her, especially those who are the closest. There are many people who struggle with their lives because of childhood conditions, and they manage as best they can. They are with us right now, sharing this time and space. They are frightened and unhappy, and they sit next to you in the beauty salon.

How will you know them? Well, if you feel a sudden irritation at the back of your throat and have an incredible urge to start hacking...need I say more?

Angels.... where are the angels in this story?

The angels are the rest of the clients who bring so much joy into the salon that it would be impossible to tell their stories in one book. It would take me a lifetime to tell about the daily adventures we take in our conversations and the stories that we hear inside the walls of my little studio. Safe in my memory are those who are incredibly good, loving, kind, passionate, and generous people. They are not extraordinary, but normal, everyday people who live life with faith that the world is a good and safe place to live in...and they make good things happen in the world.

Many authors have made millions of dollars writing and speaking about their personal experiences with angels that are with us from places far away. Others are wishing that they too could see and communicate with those angels, and to them I say this: there are angels everywhere. They are in your family, in your workplace, in your neighborhood and community, and they are real people just like you and me. You don't have to go far to find a human angel. You just have to be open to their presence.

My neighbor, who at one time irritated the hell out of me for his "know it all, be in everybody's business" attitude, has become the angel across the street who pays close attention to everything in the neighborhood. (Okay, I might be stretching on that one, but he really is a good man....just inquisitive, and it serves the neighborhood well.)

Everywhere you look, there are people helping others. Get to know those you work with. Volunteer with charitable institutions, support the shelters for those less fortunate, and join a spiritual center that rings your chimes. Decide to feed your soul, lighten your heavy load and introduce hope to those frightened spaces in your thoughts.

When you do discover the angels around you, please do not expect them to be perfect human beings. These angels have their own stuff they are dealing with. More often than not, that is why they have chosen to help others. Angels are everywhere....

Snip-It

In 1996 while attending a weeklong seminar facilitated by Jack Canfield at the University of Santa Barbara, a group of us volunteered to become readers for the now well-known *Chicken Soup for the Soul* book series. Jack Canfield and his staff were collecting hundreds of stories from people throughout the country that would be added to *A 4th Course of Chicken Soup for the Soul*.

As the official panel of readers, we would receive in the mail a large packet of stories that we were to read and score using a scale from one to ten, ten being the best. The only instructions we received were to read each story, use our own judgment as to how each story touched our soul, rate the stories, and send back the paperwork as soon as possible.

Within a week of the seminar, I received my package of stories to read. Since I was working long hours in the salon, I decided to bring the stories with me and read them in between clients. I had no idea how much these stories would grab my feelings and distract me from my workday. It was impossible to sit for a moment and try to read just one story, rate it, and then get up and try to work on a client. Most of the time I was crying and totally taken in by the sincere offering of the writer. Other times I laughed so hard that I had to excuse myself and run *carefully* to the bathroom. Reading in the evenings was out of the question. I was too tired to stay awake, and all that emotional stuff kept me up too late. Anyway, it wasn't going as smoothly as I thought it would, and I was running out of time to get the stories read, rated, and mailed back.

I had promised myself to complete the readings on this particular day at work. I thought it was going to be a lighter than usual schedule, and I would have plenty of time between clients to finish the stack I had left.

As it happened, the day did not lend itself to reading until my last client walked in the door. Rick was a handsome, tall (six foot, five inch), playful, broadly built, "macho type" of man. A "man's man," he was also quite a woman's man. Jokes were his thing and the dirtier they were the more he liked telling them. Having never been married at the age of forty-five, he had been around the block—parties, beds, and relationships—many, many times.

On this particular day, he was in for his low light, or what we also call a reverse weave, and a haircut. Because he was almost completely grey, I painted thin, dark streaks throughout his full head of hair using long strips of foil. The result is natural. Instead of being grey all over, he looks as if he is just beginning to turn silver.

After placing the foils in his hair, I sent him to sit in the dryer chair away from the front of the salon. He would be the only client and that would give me plenty of time to read. He could sit and look through the magazines. I placed a small stack of Chicken Soup Stories on my station, excused myself, and went to the restroom.

Upon my return, I found Rick sitting at the drying chair reading from the stack of Chicken Soup Stories. He looked up at me and asked, "It's okay, isn't it?" I thought for a moment and said, "Why not! I won't tell if you don't. Enjoy, and let me know what you think."

I took the stories that were left on my station and sat in my chair facing the mirror. I could see Rick to my right as we sat quietly reading.

After a while I could see that he had moved the pages from his lap up to the front of his face. Then I thought I heard sniffling… I knew I heard sniffling.

I sat for a bit longer and very slowly and quietly walked over to where he was reading. Unnoticed, I stood watching and listening, thinking how silly he looked in his foils, t-shirt, shorts and sneakers sitting in a hair salon. Big, handsome playboy—what would his drinking buddies think? I looked over his pages down at his face, and I could see his tear-filled eyes. As he looked up at me, the tears released and rolled down his cheeks.

"You big baby," I said to him. "Look at you sitting here, crying. Aren't you embarrassed?"

"Nope…I'm not," he answered.

I took the stack of stories in my hand and hit his arm with them. We laughed and then teamed up as reading partners. We sat for the next hour, reading and scoring the stories together. It was way cool, and it revealed a side of him that I didn't know existed. Underneath the bravado and all of the dirty jokes and nasty comments, Rick was a *Chicken Soup for the Soul* kind of guy.

Shrink At The Sink
No More

I was at the end of my day on Friday, finishing my last client from a long, busy week. My assistant had gone home early, and I was ready to go home myself when I answered the ringing phone. The woman on the other end was breathless, and, by the tone of her voice, upset.

Speaking like an auctioneer at a fast-paced auction she said, "My neighbor gave me your name and number. She said that you would know what to do with my hair. It's a mess, and I don't know if there's anything that you can do. Can you help me?"

"Slow down and tell me with as much detail as you can what has happened," I replied.

Nervously, her voice dripping with apprehension, she continued, "I was bleaching my hair today in my kitchen, just like I do the first and third Friday of every month, when my ex-boyfriend started banging on my front door. I've been trying to break up with him for weeks, but he won't listen. He doesn't believe that I'm finished and that this relationship is over. I'm done with him and I don't ever want to see him again. After dating him for a year, I've had it with his jealousy and that controlling thing he does."

"Okay," I said, letting her know that I was still on the other end of the line.

She continued. "I had applied the bleach to my hair and was waiting for the last five minutes to get in the shower and shampoo the bleach out when he started the banging. It was so loud that I had to answer it. I live in a townhouse and both my sidewalls are connected to my neighbors on each side. He was yelling that he needed to talk to me right away. I hung up the phone on him this morning and asked him never to contact me again, and now he was outside my front door.

"Anyway, I wrapped my head with a kitchen dish towel that was handy—the bleach was still on my head—and opened the door. I told him I was about to get in the shower and that I couldn't talk to him. But he insisted that he was not going to leave until we talked about getting back together again. I replied, 'Go away! I have to get in the shower now and leave for work in less than an hour.'

"It was one o'clock in the afternoon when all of this was happening and I had to leave for work by two. I work the late shift at a restaurant, and I don't get out until eleven at night. He knew my schedule, but he was not going to give up.

"He told me that he would lie down behind my car, which was in the carport, and that I would have to run over him when I left for work, saying that he would rather die than lose me. I was sure the neighbors could hear every word he was saying. I watched as he walked to the back of my car and lay down on the cement across the back wheels of the car. How stupid is that!"

"Okay, I'm still listening," I said hoping that she would get to the hair soon, although at this point, I had a pretty good idea what had happened to her hair. It was seven o'clock in the evening, and I was beyond exhaustion. I thought of hanging up, but I didn't know who the neighbor was who had recommended her to me. It was a little touchy.

She continued, "I walked outside and tried to talk him out of making such a fool of himself, but he wouldn't listen. He actually scooted himself all the way in under the center of the car.

"I was still not willing to let him come inside my home. I would never be able to get him out. He's one of those men who are painfully, pathetically, needy. You know the type? They just suck the life right out of you. My girlfriends tried to warn me about using the Internet dating service, but I didn't listen."

She took a deep breath and continued, "Anyway, Mrs. Caruthers, who lives next door on the east side of my house, who is eighty-five, came out to see what was going on. She asked me if I needed help. I told her what was going on, and she looked underneath my car. There he was. She suggested that I call the police, to which my boyfriend replied, 'If you call the police, I'll tell them to search your home for that stash of good stuff that you keep hidden in the bottom drawer of your nightstand in your bedroom.' Mrs. Caruthers wanted to know what stash he was talking about and I told her I had no idea. The neighbor on the other side of my house, a retired social worker, came out next to see what all the noise was about."

By now, I had put the phone on my shoulder and was trying to press it up to my ear as I worked faster to finish my last client. I was more than ready to go home. "Why don't you just tell me how your hair looks right now, and we can skip the rest of the story?" I interrupted.

"Actually, Mr. Roberts, the retired social worker, who is in his late seventies, tried to talk him out from under the car. I thought that for sure he would come out, but after a couple of hours, he was still not willing to give up his position under the car or his decision about us getting back together again.

"At four o'clock I finally called the police. By that time I had called in sick to work and I had someone filling in for me. We waited for the police to arrive, and they knew he wasn't armed or anything, but they didn't want to force him out. He was talking normally with them, and he actually knew one of the officers. They had grown up together, and they started talking about some of the pranks that they used to do when they were growing up wild in the farmlands of Illinois.

"Mrs. Caruthers brought out some lemonade for everyone, except for my boyfriend, Stewart, who was still under the car. She had also made some of my favorite chocolate chip cookies that morning, and she brought them out to give everyone. By now most of the neighbors were out in my front yard waiting to see what the police would do with Stewart."

I tried to interrupt again. My client had left. It was dark outside, and I had cleaned up my salon and was ready to go home. "Excuse me," I said loudly. "What is your name?"

"Oh, my name is Roslyn," she said quickly.

"Well, Roslyn, I don't know what I can do for you at this hour, but tell me this—have you shampooed your hair yet?"

"No, I'm afraid to at this point. My hair is hard and stiff, and the dishtowel is stuck to it. It's been on for seven hours, and now I'm afraid to put water on it. Do you think it's going to melt and wash down the drain when I wet it?" she asked.

I answered, "Well, I'm not sure what it will do. My guess is that it will go down the drain. But here is the really good news for you, Roslyn. Your hair will grow back again."

I heard her draw a quick breath of surprise, and then there was silence.

Interrupting the silence I asked, "What happened to Stewart?"

"Well, Stewart went away with the police to the court house. He called me a few minutes ago, and he's coming by to talk. I told him I would listen, but only if he promised to behave and leave early. My best friend came over for awhile, and she just left to go home. We're all beat from the day. I need to get to bed and get a good night's sleep."

"Okay," I said next. "That sounds like a great idea. Now who is the neighbor who recommended me to you?"

"Well, the truth is, I have been carrying your name with me on a napkin for about a month. Someone that was in for dinner at the restaurant one night had a great hair cut that I really liked. I asked her for her hairdresser's name and phone number and she gave it to me. I don't have any idea who the woman was and haven't seen her again in the restaurant. I have actually been cutting and bleaching my own hair for years. I thought it might be time to go to a stylist for a change."

Now irritated, I replied, "Well, Roslyn, there is nothing that I can do for you tonight whether your hair falls out or not. My suggestion for this evening is to get into the shower and get that bleach off your head, and my suggestion for tomorrow...."

(In the Introduction I mentioned Tammy, Wayne, and

136

Jon, whom I worked with at different salons during my career. Each one had recommended that I not continue in the hair business. None of them thought I had the talent for it. At this moment, I was thinking that they might be right.

I had heard that Tammy had stopped doing hair and was now shoeing horses. Wayne and Jon were working in salons not far from where I worked, and I happened to have their phone numbers. This would be a great opportunity for either one of them to really shine.)

"Tomorrow, Roslyn, you might want to call one of these fine hairstylists. Either one will be able to help you. They are the very best in the field." I gave Roslyn both numbers and wished her luck with her hair and with Stewart.

She Loves Me,
She Loves Me Not

There are two types of people—those who love their hair, and those who don't. Those who don't love their hair—no matter how superb the texture, the richness of the color, the thickness of each strand, or how manageable it is—are people who are unhappy with life in general. Their personal slogan is that life is difficult and unfair. These folks enjoy poor health, living in crisis, and, in general, they thrive on a regular diet of complaints and blame.

The fortunate ones who do love their hair—no matter how fine each skinny, little strand, how unmanageable the cowlick, how stubborn the gun-metal grey, or even the most dreaded of all, male pattern baldness—if they still love their hair, these are the best people to be with! They take life with a savoir-faire, come-as-it-may, no-big-deal, it-will-work-out attitude, doing the best they can with what they have and enjoying life instead of complaining or blaming.

Sherry loves her hair.

My friend Sherry has fine, thin hair. When we first met over thirty years ago, her hair was on its way out...or better said, on its way off her head from over-bleaching.

Most women who start bleaching their hair at a very young age, in high school or even elementary school, are in for a huge surprise by the time they reach thirty. The hair becomes compromised from over-bleaching, the scalp becomes irritated and over-sensitive to the elements, and each application of bleach and toner goes directly into the blood stream and is processed through the organs.

Fortunately, through years of research and demand for better quality, hair products have improved dramatically.

Believe me, I attended cosmetology school when the dinosaurs were still walking the earth. Products have improved and have set a new, healthier standard for hair-care and body absorption of chemicals. Some manufacturers are creating organic products, which are my favorites, and if you don't think it matters that they are organically formulated, start thinking otherwise.

My point to this is that Sherry now has fabulous hair. She is one of those fortunate ones who love life no matter what happens, and she has the same feelings toward her hair. Over the years we have worked together and have made conscious choices about her hair care. For example, instead of bleaching on the scalp, we now highlight with foils off the scalp, and we use only organic products. We use buffered bleaches and colors and keep a thorough record of any changes. Her hair is still fine and thin, but now it is manageable and shiny and grows like a weed.

During the years, Sherry's life has had its up and downs. She has been married, divorced, remarried, and has raised children. A community-minded, hard-working, active woman, she has involved herself in projects such as the Fiesta Bowl and has served on a number of public boards in the city. In her personal life, she is an avid tap dancer, tennis enthusiast, wife, mother, devoted daughter, and great friend to many. Sherry is the most uniquely loving, open-minded, kind-hearted individual that I have ever met. She loves her hair!

In our thirty years together, I have never heard her say one unkind word about anyone…. ever. Not even one tiny complaint, or blame, or judgment has ever come from her lips. I truly wish I could say the same about myself.

Years ago, while Sherry was still single, she moved with her gentleman friend to Colorado. It was a sad good-bye for both of us. I knew that I would miss her monthly appointments and especially our conversations. But she had made the decision to make the move with him.

A couple of months after she left, she called to make an appointment. Sherry was having trouble finding a hairdresser that she liked in Colorado. For the next six months, she flew back monthly to Arizona, and we continued to take care of her hair in the salon. I am sure her hair wasn't the only reason that she was making the trips back and forth. Since she felt very close to her family and friends, she wanted to remain intimately connected to all of us.

One year into her commuting, Sherry made an announcement: "I've been able to replace my favorite grocery store, manicurist, dance studio and tennis club, and I've also replaced my doctors, including the dentist and gynecologist, but I've not been able to replace my hairdresser. I'm moving back home!"

Greta hates her hair.

Greta came to the salon recommended by a mutual friend who promised her that she would not only love her haircut and style, but that she and I would have lots in common to talk about, and we would unquestionably enjoy each other's company.

Of course, Greta had fabulous hair. Not only was it thick, shiny, wavy, and a stunning shade of dark auburn, but she had yet to begin graying as she moved toward her fortieth birthday. This head of hair had everything great going for it, and she would be an easy client to take care of.

While I was at the sink washing her hair, she shared that she was turning forty in a few days and that she had planned a birthday party at her home. She had invited nineteen women to help her celebrate. Our birthdays were exactly six months apart. I was six months older.

While working on her hair, I also discovered that she held a PhD in communications, owned her own consulting business, loved to travel, was single, had never been married, and loved dogs. She also admitted that she hated her hair, and that after going to hundreds of stylists throughout the years, she was about ready to give up looking for anyone to do it right! There is something about that statement that automatically makes my hands sweat and my heart pound. Anyway, I was going to give it my best shot!

Not wanting to be a statistic or, at the least, the next notch on her bedpost for bad hairdressers, I took my time and tried my best to give her the best hair cut she had ever had. How could I go wrong? I thought to myself. Greta's hair was gorgeous. There was no way to screw it up. A blind person could give her a haircut and come out winning. A slightly layered "bob" was a no-brainer...or so I thought.

At the end she wasn't sure if she liked it.

Trying desperately to convince her to give herself time to adjust to the new cut, I persuaded her that after the first washing and blow drying at home, she would love the new style, and I accepted her invitation to attend her birthday party the following Saturday.

Greta's home was charming and well-decorated. As a world traveler, she had collected precious artifacts, including ceremonial masks, beaded garments, and other *objects d'art* that adorned her walls and shelves. Her home was truly a masterpiece of art and cleverness. I was impressed by her excellent taste in choosing color and textures that complemented each other. From what I could tell, her girlfriends all appeared to be like her—bright and worldly.

Aside from our mutual friend, Anna-Maria, a part-time psychic and full-time schoolteacher, I knew no one. Fortunately, the rest of the women were friendly and included me in the conversations.

After we all walked around the buffet table and filled our plates with an array of delicious munchies, we gathered in the great room to talk and eat. Having a sweet tooth, I couldn't help but perk up when I heard talk about the flourless "chocolate on chocolate" cake with mousse filling and frosting that was going to be served for dessert. From where I sat, I could see it on the kitchen counter placed royally on a beautiful crystal pedestal.

Greta asked us to introduce ourselves to the rest of the women now sitting in a circle on chairs, sofa, and cushioned benches. The women began their introductions. They were all highly educated with degrees in business, computer science, social work, human resources and medicine. The introductions went fairly fast, no one taking too much time on themselves, especially since they already knew about each other through Greta. The introductions were mostly for my benefit, and I was grateful.

Being the last one to introduce myself, I finished by saying that I had cut and styled Greta's hair that week and that I was glad to see her looking so great that evening with her new "do." Everyone immediately turned to look at her and caught the disillusioned look on her face as she announced, "I'm not happy with it!"

Have you ever felt the urge to disappear? Have you ever wanted to melt into the floor like old wax fades into wood, never to be seen again? Well, that is exactly how I felt. Greta hated her hair.

Changing the conversation, one of the women asked Greta if she was still seeing her long time, on-again, off-again friend. They had met while working for the same company, before Greta started her own business. He had been the head of the department that she had worked in. After she had left the company, they became a couple. Their relationship spanned twenty years, mostly not seeing each other, but always coming back to try again. In between the on-again, off-again courtship, they had each dated other people.

This is where the evening took a turn in a direction that I never expected. One of the women, the one in medical supply sales, began telling a story about the time that she and Greta got even with some man who had screwed them over.

According to the story, she and Greta had both dated the same man at the same time and didn't know it. He used his first name, Jesse, while dating Greta and his middle name, James, while dating the other woman and used a completely different last name for both. He was Jesse Allen for Greta and James Archer for her.

The story sounded like a B-grade Hollywood movie. I will spare you the gory details. But after lots of flowers, cards, hot and steamy sex in every room in his home and in his Corvette, the love affair was over for both of them, and at about the same time. Did I forget to mention that he had borrowed money from each of them? Of course, it was a loan. He was waiting for a huge check that was coming in from some business deal. He needed just a bit to hold him over.

He had convinced them that it would be embarrassing for anyone to know about this. It was the first time that he had ever borrowed money from anyone. Yeah, right!

One evening when the women were meeting for a happy hour drink at a new restaurant, they both saw him sitting at the bar. To their surprise, they discovered that they had been dating the same man. Surprise might not be a strong enough word here, but it will do. They talked over the entire unpleasant situation: the sex, the promises, the borrowed money, and the lies he had told them about who he was.

Sitting at a corner table, they watched him as he worked the bar. Like a snake slithering around the women, working his way in and out of conversations, searching out his next innocent victim, he pounced on one, and his seductive dance began.

Both Greta and her friend knew exactly what would happen next. They had both had the same experience. First of all, he would proceed to get the new prey drunk enough that she could not walk without his help. He would insist on walking her to his car, the Corvette, where she would be impressed by his great taste in cars. He would then promise to drive her home safely...but first a little drive to lover's mountain for a spectacular view of the city. Afterward, he would take her to his home where he would sit with her on the sofa and serve her cheese, fruit, chocolate, and more to drink. In the meantime he would fill the bathtub with lots of sudsy, hot water for a seductive bath. The rest would be history. God only knew how many women he had seduced in that very same manner, and each seduction had the same ending. She was just one more mouse for this snake.

Greta and her friend continued telling the story as we all listened with anticipation.

As the two women sat in the bar getting angrier with him and themselves for allowing such a stupid thing to happen, they decided on revenge! Being careful not to be noticed, they sneaked out of the restaurant and headed out to his home. It was payback time!

After arriving at his home, they would have about forty-five minutes before he brought his little mouse home for a bath. On the drive out to the house, they master-planned their retribution, and it was going to be a good one.

His home had a basement, a main floor with a living room, a kitchen, and a den. On the upper floor were two bedrooms and a loft. The bathtub was located in his master bedroom.

There was a window that led to the basement where the laundry area was situated. This was also where all the water pipes were located. This would be the scene of the crime.

As the women at the party listened to the story, bottles of wine were passed around the circle several times. There was a sense of excitement while Greta and her friend recounted the series of events that followed.

Back in the basement, Greta found a large hammer with a long handle, and her friend picked up a crowbar that was on a workbench. At the count of three, making sure that the path was clear to the window for a quick escape, they began smashing the water pipes, including the ones that were connected to the hot water tank. The water gushed quickly, and began to fill the floor of the basement. In their high heels, pulling up their skirts, they made a dash for the window and got out.

Laughing all the way home, they could only imagine what he would do when he tried to fill the tub. The next day would be even worse when he would have to estimate the cost of fixing things. Neither Greta nor her friend felt any thing but justified.

It took a while for the party group to stop laughing. They howled and cheered and made comments about wishing they could have been there. They thought that what was done was well-warranted and that he needed to be taught a lesson.

Another woman in the group threw her hand up and yelled, "My turn, my turn! I want to go next!"

Her story was similar, about a man who had cheated on her. Her way of getting even was hiring two young boys to take a sledgehammer to his BMW while it was parked at his gym. They were paid to smash the windows and slash the tires.

I looked over at Anna-Maria and wondered how she was feeling. Pretty damn sober is how I was feeling. I looked over at the cake and wished that they would serve it now. But from the looks of things and the fact that yet another woman was yelling that she also had a story of revenge that was even better, the cake was going to sit there on its crystal pedestal for a long time to come.

After her story, which had to do with the ruination of her cheating man's credit scores, the women began to share titles of books that had lists of ways to get even. I sat wondering why I wasn't laughing and finding this story-telling funny. Was something wrong with me? Was I a passive-aggressive person, and, instead of outwardly getting even, was I less obvious when I felt revengeful? Greta had not liked her haircut. Would she be getting even with me? I would have to skip the flourless "chocolate on chocolate" cake.

The conversation was still going on and the women were having a great time talking about the getting-even books when I stood up, walked into the kitchen, and placed my plate in the sink.

I then put my finger in the cake and tasted the most delicious, decadent dessert that I have ever tasted in my life, and, as quietly as possible, I left.

As I was getting into my car, Anna-Maria caught up with me. "You're leaving?" she asked hesitantly, more of a statement than a question.

"I am," I answered.

"I don't blame you. I wish I could leave also," she said as her voice trailed softly.

"Why don't you?" I asked.

"I'm afraid that I'll be next to be talked about. I wish I had your guts!" she said.

"I'm not sure if it's guts that I have," I answered, "but I know one thing...I love my hair!"

If you are curious about my observation of those who love their hair and those who don't, ask around. You might be amazed and amused. And how about you? How do you feel about your hair? Be honest!

What Goes Around,
Comes Around,
Stays Around

Ageless, elegant, and flawless is how I describe Evelyn Macy. She first walked into the salon as if she owned the place. Medium height, slender, early fifties, short, thick blonde hair perfectly coifed with a double-weave that accentuated her light golden highlights with a background of soft caramel brown. A woman with the style and carriage of a high-fashion model, all eyes fell quickly on her as she entered the room and announced who she was and that she was early for her hair appointment. *Yeah!*

It was not only her white, pink-trimmed St. John knit skirt and sweater, her eye-catching jewelry, or her absolutely striking face; it was an unmistakable attitude of confidence that Evelyn exuded that captured the attention of the other women in the salon. Like the opening drum roll at a long- awaited performance, all conversation stopped and heads turned to face her.

After acknowledging her, I asked Evelyn to have a seat in the lobby and to fill out the customary client form. (We don't actually have a lobby. It's two chairs in a hallway, two steps from the doorway. Rarely does it bother me to have several clients inside the salon at one time, but at this moment I felt rather intimidated by Evelyn's presence.)

I assured her that we would be with her in a few minutes. I peeked over at the appointment book to see what hair services Evelyn was having and noticed it was only a blow dry. That could mean several things: she was visiting from out of state; she was replacing her local hairdresser and was evaluating my skill level; she was from the Arizona State Board of Cosmetology scrutinizing our business practices; or she was from the IRS. (Of *course* we report all our tips!) Either way we were prepared.

After a few minutes and seeing that she had completed the client form, I took a deep breath and invited her in.

"I'd like a shampoo and blow dry today. Just freshen me up," said Evelyn as she sat in my chair. "I don't need anything fancy. I simply need a fresh style for this evening and I don't feel like doing it myself," she continued. Immediately, I knew this was not the truth, but I didn't have enough information yet to decide why she was really there. "It will be my pleasure," I answered, motioning to Michelle, who was already standing by the shampoo chair ready to get Evelyn started.

Wet hair is like a hallucinogenic drug. Barriers of secrecy are washed away during the shampoo process, and I have witnessed people lose their crust of protection as their hair is rinsed. The body sits motionless, hands resting on the lap. The soothing hypnotic feel of hands and comb or brush stroking the hair and scalp create a safe place for release. In a matter of moments after entering the hair salon, people's life stories are dispersed like dandelion seeds on a summer breeze. Years of privacy are left behind, and, like the earth's seasons, each person moves through the story in a variety of expressions.

Some lives are more colorful than others; some are cold with restricted minds that direct every thought and hold back from full expression; others are heated with passion and danger as their lives play like an unforgettable love scene in a classic movie masterpiece. One client after another, we listen and watch as the stories unfold.

After her shampoo, as she sat in my chair again, I combed and applied gel to Evelyn's wet hair and set the dryer on the quiet, low speed. Evelyn began, "We have mutual friends who suggested that I see you. I had dinner with John and Carrie Doors last week. Carrie said that I would enjoy talking with you. I'm here because I have a problem that I've been dealing with for most of my adult life and I can't stand to carry it around with me any longer."

Positioning myself closer to Evelyn, I proceeded to slowly blow-dry her hair. Looking at her face in the mirror, I acknowledged what she had said as our eyes connected and we came to an understanding that she had all my attention. "I am depressed," she continued. "I can't remember what it feels like not to be depressed. Carrying the weight of a heavy, dark cloud in my body is the only feeling that I recognize, and it continues to weigh me down. At times, I observe myself welling up like a bad storm about to let loose, and then nothing happens. I'm paralyzed and unable to let myself express the full force of my emotions. I crumble and tuck everything back inside myself, and I do nothing. I do nothing but wait. And nothing happens, except more depression.

"One doctor after another has put me on medication, and they have all told me there is nothing else that can be done. A year ago, out of desperation to get off the medication, I immersed myself in the study of alternative remedies for depression. Devouring everything that I could get my hands on, I have learned much about the illness and, consequently, I have discovered a lot about myself. After reading books about the power of the mind and how the body is a manifestation of our thoughts, beliefs, and emotions, and after researching my family medical history, I'm convinced that I must change my thoughts, beliefs, and emotions to get well."

Evelyn drew a long breath and sat quietly for a moment before she continued. I continued blow-drying, a style now beginning to take shape as I moved from one area of her head to the other. Evelyn continued. "Recently I read a book by Louise Hay, *Heal Your Body*, where she writes about the "Mental Equivalents," what we know to be our continual thought patterns and how our thoughts create our life experiences, both good and bad. In her book, she explains that every thought we have results in something. Every effect in our life is preceded by a thought pattern. Good things come from good thoughts, and disease is created by those thoughts that are negative and dishonoring to our health. In essence, we create what we think about continually. When I read her theory about self-creating illnesses, it made sense to me.

"I know that my depression won't simply disappear immediately by changing my thoughts and repeating the affirmations that she talks about, but it is a beginning. I know it is important for me to take some responsibility for keeping this depression alive and well-fed. Understandably, it will take time, commitment and discipline to change the thoughts I have held for over fifty years, but I'm having trouble getting started with the process. I want desperately to change my life and leave the depression behind before it eats me alive."

Only the sound of the hair dryer filled the room as Evelyn became quiet. My mind held on to her statement, "before it eats me alive."

It had been years since I too had read Louise Hay's book, but I was still familiar with the theory of "Mental Equivalents." It had been very helpful for me many years back when I had suffered with anxiety and panic disorder. Reading the book over and over again until I had memorized the affirmations, it eventually helped me release my anxiety. It had kept me calm during those times of unbearable fear. I had recommended it to many others who I thought would resonate with the concept. And for many, as it was for me, it had been a catalyst for a new, healthier life.

"Can you tell me what it says in the book about the cause of depression?" I asked.

Evelyn, feeling certain of her response, answered confidently, *"Anger you feel you do not have a right to have."*

"And what is the affirmation?" I asked.

Evelyn answered, *"I now go beyond other people's fears and limitations. I create my life."*

The words sounded so familiar. I remembered how much I had clung to similar affirmations myself. I also recalled how I had struggled, thinking that I had to learn to love and accept myself before I could heal my anxiety. I wondered if Evelyn was feeling the same hopelessness. After all, depression and anxiety are very close cousins which attack and paralyze an individual's self-worth. I remembered the feelings all too well.

Continuing to make eye contact with her in the mirror, I asked, "Evelyn, how do you feel about the statement, '*Anger you feel you do not have a right to have?*'"

Starting to fidget and looking down, our eye contact gone from the mirror, she looked at the folds of the cape covering her hands on her lap. Evelyn muttered, "It makes me sick to my stomach. I want to shut down even further than where I am normally."

Our salon was empty. Two clients were on their way out when Evelyn arrived, and Michelle had taken a well-deserved break. This was one of those times when I was grateful to work in a single-person salon. We were alone.

"Take a deep breath, Evelyn, and stay present in this room. It is you and I, and we are having a conversation. My purpose is to listen, and there is no judgment. I am simply listening. Take a deep breath, and I will breathe with you."

Evelyn took her time as she gathered enough small bits of air in her mouth to take a deep breath. Slowly, as her head came up and her shoulders moved back, she breathed in deeply and calmed herself into a long and steady inhale. In unison, we slowly exhaled and smiled at each other in the mirror.

Remembering a sensation I had on a cruise ship in the Hawaiian Islands, I could feel myself standing with my face toward the fresh air that rushed over the bow of the ship. At that moment I felt as if I were clearing my mind for the first time in my life. I tried to imagine that Evelyn and I could take in that amount of fresh air right now to clear our minds.

"How long have you been off the medication?" I asked.

"About eleven months," Evelyn answered.

"Who are you angry with?" I asked.

"It's my mother, Mildred. She emotionally abandoned me when I was five. No matter what I said or did, I could never be enough for her. Never meeting her expectations, I was starved for her attention, love, and approval. To this day, I continue to hold on to the belief that I am not enough. Now my hunger has turned to depression. As I have delved deeper into alternative medicine and the power of the mind, something deep inside me remembers when I shut myself down and began feeling the weight of my mother's abandonment. I know all of this, but I can't seem to stop myself from having the feelings of

152

anger toward her. The anger seems to grow. I feel it in my stomach.

"I also understand that I must let go of what happened in the past and take full responsibility for my reactions toward Mother, who is still alive and doing very well.

"She recently moved to California to be near my younger sister, Janie, and my three children who live there. They are very close."

Listening to Evelyn's words, I could tell that she had indeed been reading alternative healing books. Taking responsibility for the way we respond to our life circumstances is the foundation of most self-help teachings.

"I see there is a lot work left to do around your mother," I said. "My work was around my father, and forgiving him was the last stage for me as I worked on healing my anxiety. I understand how you feel."

Only the rhythmic sound of the blow dryer continued to fill the space in the room. We were silent as I stood behind the chair, waiting for her to continue.

Her last visit to the psychiatrist had been a year ago when she announced that she was stopping the medication. The psychiatrist had advised her to continue the medication and not think that the alternative methods of natural herbs, mind power, or "hocus-pocus new age stuff" were going to heal her depression. He warned her that it could be dangerous to stop the medication.

Evelyn's history with medication began when she started taking Valium for depression at the age of thirty-two when her last child was born. At the age of forty-five, her doctor changed her prescription to Xanax. Several years later, addicted to Xanax and alcohol, Evelyn had been hospitalized for detoxification, at which point she was given Prozac.

A year ago, on her final visit to her psychiatrist, she told him that at fifty-eight she was determined to find a better way to live than to be medicated for depression the rest of her life. She had been wary of the dull sensations of being artificially numb. The psychiatrist expressed his disappointment and disapproval as she left his office.

Evelyn continued, "I want to get to the core of the problem. I've been told that it may be a psychological, chemical problem, but I don't think so. No one in my family has ever been diagnosed with depression or anxiety or any other mental disorder. We are a sturdy stock of English and Welsh farmers, solid in our mental health. We are those hard-working, hearty, fun-loving people who don't hoard anything, including how we feel about things, except for my mother who was simply spoiled and protected by my father, which made her selfish and difficult to get along with. But she was not mentally ill.

I honestly don't think depression is genetic in my family, but I do think that I have to make a definite change in my attitude and my thought process. And that is the struggle. Trying to let loose of this thing that holds me back is like being tied to a chair at a fantastic party and watching everyone else dancing and having fun. I think the hunger for being seen for who I am and not who I have created over the years to cover up my emptiness is what I am ready to let go of. Am I making sense to you?"

I thought of the feelings of intimidation that I had felt earlier when Evelyn had walked into my salon and how her own unworthiness was well-hidden behind her confident facade. Her offense—to look fabulous—was her best defense, and it appeared to be working.

"Of course you are making sense. I hear you loud and clear, and, as I said earlier, I understand how you feel, and I am here to listen."

I could hear Michelle's footsteps coming down the hallway. I was now finished styling Evelyn's hair, and as she remained seated, I asked her, "How long has it been since you have had a complete medical check up? Are your hormone levels in check? Is your thyroid gland functioning well? Have you seen a doctor for any problem other than the depression?" (Who knew that hairdressing would include taking a health history from a client?)

Evelyn explained that she had had a hysterectomy three years previously and that before entering the hospital they had given her a pre-op examination. "I'm actually very healthy. I rarely catch a cold or any other virus floating around. The only ache I have is my lower back and a persistent upset stomach, which I blame on all of the driving around that I do in my business. I'm a real estate agent, and lately I have been very busy. I drive around all day with clients getting in and out of the car, and at times I skip meals or eat unhealthy fast foods to get to the next appointment. It has taken a toll on my body. I've been walking every morning and stretching in the evenings and trying to carry a healthy snack with me instead of eating something full of chemicals, but nothing seems to help. I've been putting off going to see my doctor. I hate having to tell him that I'm off my medication."

I took the styling cape off to signify that our time together was over, and Evelyn stood up to pay her bill. "I would like to come in again next week if you don't mind," she asked.

"That would be just fine," I answered.

I walked Evelyn down the hallway as she left. "I will listen to your story, and I will pay attention to see what questions are still left unanswered by that part of you that knows what you must do. I will accept you unconditionally with no judgment, and I will style your hair beautifully. Is that enough for you, Evelyn?" I asked.

"Yes. I want to tell you my story. I feel as if something good can happen for me in this place. I felt it the minute I walked in the door."

At her second appointment, Michelle gave her the last appointment of the day so that no one else would be in the salon. Evelyn shared two distinctive periods of her childhood: before her baby sister was born, and after her baby sister was brought home from the hospital. She was five, and at that point her world "turned upside down." Or at least that was how she remembered the birth of baby Janie.

"The day Janie came home from the hospital, I became invisible to Mother. I had heard Mother talk about her experience with me during my infant years. She would say that I had been difficult in every way. To begin with, I was born premature and jaundiced. I was a colicky baby and cried all the time, and then I developed severe ear infections. It seemed as if I went from one medical problem to another. Not even my teeth came in without difficulty, and, at the age of three, I had to wear leg braces. I was severely bowlegged, causing my feet to protrude outward. I wore those braces for two years and because Mother thought that the more I wore them the faster I could get them off, she made me sleep in them at night. 'She was difficult from the very beginning,' I heard Mother say about me to anyone who would listen.

"But when Janie was born, she was perfect. Sleeping the entire night and only waking up for meals, diaper changes, and smiling at Mother, Janie was indeed the ideal child.

"Two months before she was born, our church was having their yearly Easter Sunday picnic. It seemed as if the entire town came together to celebrate. Everyone brought food, drinks, games, and beautifully colored, decorated eggs, along with baskets for the Easter egg hunt. It was the most festive, fun event of all the church socials we attended.

"Mother had made me the most special dress. It was white with tiny pink polka dots all over. The sleeves were full and puffy. She had starched them and stuffed them with white tissue paper the night before so that they would stay full all day. Thin, half-inch eyelet lace trimmed the edge of the skirt and sleeves and the collar that lay like flower petals around my neck. Pearl buttons, lined up like corn rows in the back of the dress, were spaced perfectly and completed the dress like a work of art.

"Mother had spent hours making the dress for me, making sure that it fit flawlessly. She had taken me shopping for shoes and socks to match, and she had also made a bonnet that matched. Mother thought I looked better than anyone else there, and I agreed with her. She had given me the usual instructions not to get dirty and to stay looking nice all day, with photos being taken and all.

"I had always tried to make it up to Mother since I had been such a difficult baby, and I tried to be just the way she wanted me to be. I wanted that day to look my very best, but it was Johnny Milton who spilled the Kool-Aid on my dress.

"Johnny was playing hide and seek with the other boys and girls. I sat at the table by myself watching everyone else run around and play. I knew Mother was watching me and that I was never allowed to run like the other children. 'Girls don't behave that way,' she would say to me. 'You have to be a lady to be treated like a lady. You'll see what I mean when you get older.'

"Running in front of the bench where I was sitting and grabbing the full cup of cherry red Kool-aid from the table, Johnny lost his footing, twisted his ankle, and fell back on his bottom, tossing the cup of Kool-aid straight up into the air. It spilled all over me like a million drops of rainwater falling out of the sky. I screamed and stood up, shaking my skirt with my hands, and looked up to see Mother's face go into a look of awfulness. I started to cry and ran to her for support, but she turned and walked away. I tried to run after her, but Father stopped me and pulled me away. He said it would be best if I just left her alone for a while. I stood there with Father, crying and yelling for her to come back and take me with her, but she never looked back at me. No matter how much I cried, she just kept on walking to the other side of the park.

"Everyone else was coming over and telling me it was okay and that it wasn't my fault. Johnny's mother and father had put him in the car and were taking him home. His ankle was swelling up fast, and he was crying with his own pain. I think he felt bad about my dress."

As I listened to Evelyn's story, I was intrigued by the way her voice and rhythm of her speech pattern changed to what I am sure was the way she talked as a child. It was clearly a Southern drawl with a touch of a Midwest twang.

157

Evelyn continued, "Father put me in the back seat of the car, and we waited for Mother to join us. She had taken a walk around the park and finally came to the car. I apologized to her several times, but she pretended not to hear me. Finally, after I whimpered all the way home, Father took me inside the house to my room while Mother stayed in the car for a very long time. I took my bath and put my pajamas on, even though it was early in the day when all of this happened. I stayed in my room because Father told me that it would be the best thing to do for the rest of the day. He even brought dinner to my room. We pretended that I was sick and had to stay in bed. I had my dolls and stuffed rabbit, Benny, to keep me company. I hoped that Mother would forget the whole thing the next day, and we could go back to being right with each other at breakfast. But that didn't happen.

"It was the beginning of my loneliness. No matter how much I tried to get Mother's attention, I lost it forever that Easter Sunday, and it only became worse when, two months later, they brought Janie home from the hospital.

"Nothing was the same after that day. Although I had been a difficult baby, Mother and I basically had a good relationship. She would walk me to the bus stop every morning, and we would hold hands. Taking time to make all of my clothes and choosing just the right shoes to go with my dresses, and teaching me how to sit and eat with my fork and knife at meal time was all a game for us, and I had all of her attention. Even Father doted on me with presents and special candy on Sundays after church. But after that Easter Sunday, our lives were never the same."

During Evelyn's third and fourth appointments she described her teenage years. As her mother spent more time with Janie, who was now nine years old, Evelyn began to spend more of her time away from home. She was fourteen and in her first year of high school when she first laid eyes on Nick Storm, a sophomore. He was the all-star baseball, football, and basketball champ at their school. All the girls were after him. And why wouldn't they want to be with him? He was tall, gorgeous, athletic, and had a sexy, inviting smile. His grades were just good enough to keep him involved in sports, and his future as a college draft all-star to any university in the country was imminent. He had the world by the tail.

Evelyn's father, who drove her to school every morning, and with whom she still had a close relationship, listened to her talk about Nick Storm but did not approve of her feelings toward him.

He warned her that he was not the type of boy that he wanted for her. After all, he came from the wrong side of the tracks. He was Italian, and his parents were uneducated. The fact that the family had changed their name from some Italian spelling to Storm was enough to make Evelyn's father question their background. Cautioning her, "Don't get yourself involved in a situation that you might spend the rest of your life regretting," he would remind her of how she would disappoint her mother. But his warnings fell on deaf ears. Evelyn was determined to have Nick Storm for herself, and because she and her mother hardly had any relationship left, she no longer cared what her mother thought.

It took Evelyn three years to catch Nick's eye. By this time he had dated all her girlfriends, all the cheerleaders, and all the most popular girls on campus—and he was still the most handsome boy in school.

They began dating at the start of her junior and his senior year. Evelyn had worked hard to make herself available at dances and other activities which she knew he would be attending, and, finally, after the first back-to-school dance in September, he walked her home and kissed her.

At the age of seventeen, three months after their first kiss, Evelyn became pregnant. Nick's parents insisted that they marry. Nick would complete his senior year, get a job, and support the new family…. it was the Italian way. Nick would have to forget his dreams of attending college as an all-star athlete.

A small wedding with family and close friends attending was held during the Christmas-New Year holidays at

159

Evelyn's parents' beautiful home. Evelyn dropped out of school immediately. Nick completed high school and graduated with his classmates.

Evelyn's father owned a large construction company, and Nick went to work for his father-in-law. They moved into a small home that Evelyn's father owned as a rental property. Because her mother had not spent time preparing her for the rigors of marriage and housekeeping, Evelyn struggled with keeping up their small home, learning to cook, and trying to be a wife to her new husband. They were like children, fighting, making up, and trying to figure out how to get through each day. Money was tight, and Evelyn was tired all the time.

During her fifth month of pregnancy, she miscarried. Devastated, she became depressed and reached out to her mother, who was completely involved with Janie. She was involved in every activity imaginable. Talented in dance, sports, church activities, and drama, Janie required lots of time and attention from her mother.

Six months later, Evelyn was pregnant again. This time she would carry the baby to full term. At the age of eighteen, while all her girlfriends were buying new wardrobes for college, Evelyn gave birth to Mindy.

The expected challenges began for her and her husband, who lacked the skills for marriage and parenting. The fact that Evelyn's mother was so disappointed in her for getting pregnant and having to marry an Italian who had no formal education put even more distance between them.

This was not the first time that I had heard this life story. High school girl gets pregnant, the couple marries, husband goes to work for father-in-law, more children are born (in this case, two boys) and couple stays married for thirty-some years…. unhappily. The story is similar to many others I have heard. I'm not trying to diminish the pain that Evelyn felt over the years, but her life was not that different from others who marry in compromised circumstances and unhappily remain locked into "what seemed the best thing to do."

During her fifth and sixth appointments, Evelyn talked about her mother, Mildred's, painful childhood. Sadly, it was a life of poverty and abandonment. Without going into too much detail (that would require a second book) the story is heartbreaking. Mildred's father walked out on her mother the day Mildred was born. Mildred's mother was only eighteen years old, a child herself. A series of complicated circumstances led Mildred and her mother to live on a farm with distant relatives, a life of hard work and poverty. At the age of twenty-six, Mildred's mother died and Mildred, now eight years old, was left to be raised with the relatives. There were eleven boys in the family, and Mildred, the only girl, had to fight for her position in the family. She worked in the house and did not attend school.

At the age of sixteen, Mildred met Hank, and they were married within a year. Hank, a hardworking young man of twenty, worked for his father, who owned a construction company. Eventually the construction company became his. Mildred and Hank had struggled for years to make ends meet and worked hard at being married. Mildred had no idea how to be a wife, but she did know how to cook for a large group, how to keep a home spotless, and how to sew. It took Mildred and Hank ten years of trying to have their first baby, Evelyn.

I asked Evelyn if she could see how difficult it must have been for her mother to show her the attention that she wanted as a child. For some women, no matter what their own childhood circumstances, mothering comes to them naturally. For other women, that maternal instinct does not develop. It gets lost in the inner battle of self-doubt and fear of getting too close and being hurt by losing those they love. It's not unusual. But for the child at the receiving end of this unrequited love, it can be devastating.

"Thank God I didn't do that with my children," Evelyn said immediately. "I loved them unconditionally and didn't abandon them. I knew what it felt like not to have the love of a mother."

"I understand how you must feel," I continued. "I felt the same way with my father. Until I could see him as an innocent man, I felt the very same way. The upside to forgiving him and seeing that he could only be and do what he knew was that I was able to free myself to love myself and others at a much deeper level. It is so worth the effort to truly see your parents as innocents. Especially when we consider that our own children might see us in the same way someday. Who knows really how our children feel about us and how the mistakes that we have made in raising them will affect them. We must release our own misgivings toward those who we perceived have hurt us intentionally and see instead how we benefited from the experience."

Evelyn sat quietly in my chair. "Think about it, Evelyn, and think about releasing your mother's shortcomings and releasing your depression. It might be time for you to stop carrying your mother on your back and in your stomach."

After a long pause, Evelyn continued. "Tell me what to do, and I will do it. I am so tired of carrying her around in this hurtful, angry way. I am so tired." Evelyn sat with her head down looking at her shoes. They were beautiful, black leather…. very expensive shoes. She had the most exquisite taste. I wondered if that was something that she could thank her mother for.

As we sat for a few moments longer in quiet, I could see that she was ready for something deeper. Very carefully, I began to talk again. I asked if she would consider writing her mother a letter to thank her for all the special things that she had taught her to do and be. I knew that Evelyn had learned to sew, decorate her home, dress beautifully and, undoubtedly do a number of other things that Evelyn could think of if she allowed herself to look back over the years growing up in a family with means. Sometimes just being around lovely things can open your eyes to the appreciation and development of good taste.

This was obviously the case with Evelyn and her family. Although she said that her mother did not take the time to teach her how to do things, she was certainly exposed to them. There is also that saying that each one of us as parents has used to defend ourselves as parents: "We did the best we could with the information we had at the time." I could only imagine that Evelyn's mother might be thinking the same thing.

Agreeing that she would write the thank-you letter to her mother, listing specific qualities and capabilities that she had received from the mere fact of being her daughter, Evelyn promised to bring the letter with her to her next appointment. Because she would be traveling to visit her children in California, who lived near her mother, I would not see Evelyn for a few weeks.

Three weeks passed quickly. Proudly, Evelyn walked in the door looking stunning as always and handed me the letter. "Here," she said. "This is how I feel."

While she was having her shampoo, I sat in the hallway and opened the letter to get a quick peek at her words. Shocked, I read the first sentence. "Dear Mother, no matter how much I try, I will never forgive you for all of the horrific ways in which you have hurt me."

Each sentence became more hostile, and each word carried with it the destructiveness of anger. Listing the ways in which she had systematically learned to hate her over the years, Evelyn spared no adjectives to describe her feelings toward her mother and her sister, Janie. The letter was aggressive and cruel. Each condemning word felt like a dagger digging deeper and harder. I couldn't read another word. I closed the letter and put it back in the envelope.

Composing myself to enter the salon again, I felt shaken. Evelyn was now waiting in my chair, ready for her cut and blow-dry. Placing the letter on the counter in front of her, I took my hands and placed them on her shoulders as I steadied myself.

"Evelyn, the assignment was for you to write a thank-you letter to your mother. This is not a thank-you letter. What changed in your thinking from the time we talked until you wrote the letter?" Taking my hands off her shoulders, I reached for my shears and began cutting her hair.

"As much as I tried, I just couldn't do it. I have nothing to thank her for. I hate her, and I will never forgive her for what she did to me. Now she has stolen my children. She has turned them against me. They visit her on a regular basis. I know they do. They didn't have to tell me anything. I just knew it. They can't lie to me about not seeing her too often. She is talking to them about me, and she has made it more difficult for me to be with them. I can feel the deception."

"Evelyn, did anything specific happen while you were visiting with your children?" I asked.

Stiffening and bringing her shoulders up, Evelyn answered, "Not anything specific. I could just feel the distance from all of them. We spent lots of time together doing things and shopping and walking on the beach, but nothing that I can put my hands on. I saw my mother and sister, and we had a nice dinner at my sister's gorgeous home one evening, and we all got along just fine. But things just aren't the same between my children and me. All of this keeps my stomach on fire, and my back is killing me."

"Evelyn, would you consider seeing a doctor for a physical?"

"No. I don't want to do that. I'm fine. If only my children could see my side of the story. My mother has brain-washed them against me."

Completing the haircut and blow-dry, I sat with Evelyn at the end of her appointment, and we chatted. As respectfully as I could, I suggested that she needed to work with someone better qualified than I. I was only in my first year of working on my doctorate in counseling, I was busy being a hairdresser, and, after the weeks that we had worked together and the progress that I thought we had made, I knew that this was not something that I was qualified to handle. This beautiful woman who had spent a lifetime thinking of how much she hated her mother and creating an image for herself that would cover the anger that she felt inside needed a well-qualified professional.

Although over the years as a hairstylist-mental health provider, I had seen changes in some clients who had shared their stories, who had trusted for the first time, and who did not feel judged or condemned for things that they had done in the past, I knew this would not be one of them.

I suggested to Evelyn that she have a complete physical exam, find licensed psychologists, and continue the process of working and peeling away the layers of fear and disappointments. As much as I wanted to help, I knew by my reaction to the letter that I was not the one who could help her. We parted with a hug that day and I wished her well.

Three months passed when I received a phone message at home. Evelyn knew my work schedule in the salon and had clearly decided to call my home and leave me a message. "Hilda, it's me, Evelyn. I want you to know that I have been diagnosed with stomach cancer. It has spread to my spine and other organs. I am living with my mother in California. She is taking care of me until things change."

I listened to the message several times to make sure I didn't miss any of it. I remembered Evelyn telling me that her stomach was on fire and that her back was *killing* her. I wondered how long she had housed the cancer. I had no way of reaching her. Her Scottsdale phone had been disconnected, and there was no forwarding number. I called our mutual friends, the Doors, but they also had lost touch with her. There was no way for me to contact her.

Two more months passed and I received yet another phone message at my home during work hours. With the weakness of a broken body, her voice was slow and quiet. "Hilda, my mother is taking such good care of me. I thought that you might want to know. I love her. I love you."

Not only did I listen to this message over and over again, I could not erase it from the phone message system nor from my thoughts. I could hear her voice, and it buried itself in me like an unforgettable lyric in a song.

Six months to the day from her last appointment at the salon, I received a call from Evelyn's daughter, Christi. Once,

Evelyn had brought in a photo album to show me her family. Her two sons, in their thirties, were typical tall, dark, handsome Italian men. Christi, who had turned forty, was an exact replica of her mother. She was gorgeous just like her mother. No less beautiful were Evelyn's mother, Mildred, and her sister, Janie. The entire family looked like movie stars.

Christi began. "Mother wanted me to call you when she passed away. She died this morning at sunrise. She talked about you quite a bit and asked me to make sure you knew. She said that you would want to know. Mom was in a coma for the past few days, and she held on to a stuffed bunny that she named Benny that I bought for her when she was moved to the hospital. I'd like to meet with you when I'm in Scottsdale in a couple of weeks. I'll be there to go over her belongings and tidy up some business stuff that needs to be closed. Will you be available to meet with me?"

"Of course I will," I answered. "It would be my pleasure to meet you." I wrote down her number in California and the number of the hotel where she would be staying in Scottsdale. Christi wanted to come to the salon to meet.

I recognized her immediately. She was dressed in a fussy, frilly, feminine top and a skirt that moved as if a fan were blowing on her. Yellow, pink, and lavender moved in the fabric of her outfit like a sunny spring day. Her hair was long and blonde and bounced with unkempt curls, and her walk was relaxed and solid at the same time. She brought with her Benny, the bunny that she had bought for her mother. Somehow it looked like a natural thing for her to be carrying. We embraced in a tight hug and both began to cry as we held each other. I automatically rocked her in my arms as we stood dismissing the fact that we were standing in a public place. We found a quiet place to sit in the hallway, and I felt as if we had known each other for a long, long, time.

"I have something to talk to you about that is very difficult for me," she began.

"Tell me anything," I answered. "I'm here to listen."

"I need help dealing with my feelings toward my

166

mother. I know that she can't be here to defend herself, but the truth is, she abandoned me at a very early age. I feel angry and depressed, and I can't do anything about it. She's gone, and I can't ever be with her again, but she was never with me to begin with.

"All of my life I have felt as if Mother never approved of me and that I could never be enough to get her attention. Mother spent her life distracted, blaming Grandma for her depression. She was angry with Aunt Janie for her success. My brothers feel the same way. We will miss her, but we never had her to begin with. The three of us have felt the separation since we were very young. Instead, we connected with Grandma and Aunt Janie but had to lie about our feelings toward them. I hurt so badly for myself and my brothers that I could scream. Maybe if I did scream, that knot in my stomach would unwind and stop bothering me.

"Mother said that you were very helpful to her. She didn't tell me exactly what you talked about, but she said that she felt different after being with you. She talked about seeing the innocence in Grandma and that she had finally forgiven her."

We held a silent pause as we both took in the magnitude of the words "forgiven her."

"She said it was helpful…coming in here…to the salon."

Christi and I talked as she hung on to Benny. After an hour of sharing, Christi and I promised that we would stay in touch. She also promised me that she would continue seeing her counselor and that she would try not to rush the process. "It takes time to break a family cycle," I told her.

As I watched her leave and walk down the hallway and out the door, I couldn't help but wonder how many lives are caught in unnecessary suffering. I thought of all the ways we live in what happened in the past, tell the painful story to ourselves and others, and keep it circulating…. what goes around, comes around, stays around—unless we decide differently.

Snip-It

Martha had been a client for over twenty years when, at the age of eighty-nine, she moved into an assisted living facility. Her new home had every convenience that she could possibly want, including a hair salon. The only inconvenience was that it was located an hour from my home. After not seeing her for about three years, her daughter contacted me and asked if I would consider going by to see Martha. She said that her mother spoke of me often and would enjoy a visit with me.

When I called Martha to set up a time, we had to work around her busy schedule. I could not come by in the morning after breakfast because that was entertainment time for the residents. Lunch was served early, and, immediately afterward, they played Bingo. The only time that she had available was at two o'clock, and even then she would only have an hour. Her massage was at four, and she did not want to be late.

On my first visit, I was astounded to see how wonderful she looked. I honestly thought that she looked younger and healthier than three years prior. Martha admitted that she loved living in the facility and that she had felt a resurgence of health and vitality since moving in. It was obvious that it had been the right choice for her.

On my second visit, Martha was thrilled to see me because she wanted to discuss her funeral arrangements with me. Handing me a pencil and paper, she asked if I would take notes so that I would not forget some of the details. I listened as she went over some particulars. I asked if she had a preference for music.

She had not thought about it but said that she would give it some thought and have an answer for me on my next visit.

Assuming that she was comfortable with her death, I asked her how she felt about dying. "Oh, I'm looking forward to it. As a matter of fact, I ask God every night to take me. I am so prepared to leave."

I must admit that when she said, "I am so prepared to leave," I wondered why.

I asked, "Are you in a hurry to leave us?"

She answered, "I'm ready anytime, Hilda. I have had a good life. I have enjoyed much and have seen and done more than most. My body hurts, and I am ready to rest. My father used to say before he died, 'I am looking forward to what is next.' And I feel the same way now."

Martha's comment was sincere, and I could feel her positive attitude toward dying. This was not a depressed woman, but a woman who had come to terms with life and her limitations and who had embraced her mortality.

A week later, I received a call from Martha asking me to come by sooner than planned. She needed to talk to me about something she was thinking about, and she had also decided on the music to be played at her service. At Martha's age, things can happen at any time so I made plans to see her as soon as I could.

Walking into her room, I could see that she was happy to see me. "Well," she began, "I have the music. Here is the CD that I enjoy the most." She handed me the music to *An Affair to Remember*. "Excellent," I said to her. "This will be a big hit with all of us."

"And there is more that I want to talk about," she continued. "This is the biggest question that I want answered. I had two wonderful husbands. My first husband was a good man. With him I had my daughter. We had a good relationship, more than many women ever experience. When he died, I never thought that I would meet anyone as wonderful as he was, and then I met my second husband. You knew him, Hilda. He was a good man and a great husband, and we had many, many fine years. I missed him when he died. I loved them both for different reasons and in different ways. I was so lucky both times. My question is this: God willing, when I die, I will go to heaven. Who will I be with? Will I be with my first husband or my second husband, and will I have to choose?"

169

I answered, "Well, Martha, that's easy. When we leave this physical earth, and our physical bodies are left behind, we go only as spirits. From my understanding, spirits don't have bodies...we are simply light, unencumbered energy. We don't have the weight of worry or decision-making or thoughts that limit us in any way.

"I believe that you will be with both of your husbands and that they will welcome you lovingly. I can't imagine that you will have to decide anything. If there is no sleeping with each other, or intercourse, and if you simply exist as love energy, then I believe that you will be in a perpetual love fest...kind of like a love orgy. What do you think about that?"

With a beautiful smile on her face and a sparkle in her eyes, Martha leaned toward me and whispered, "I think I'm looking forward to it."

Epilogue
Color Me Happy

In the introduction of this book, I stated that we are all voyeurs at heart, endlessly curious about how others are living their lives—comparing, contrasting, judging, damning, or admiring. We pretend that we don't want to know, that we are not interested, but the truth is—WE ARE! Sometimes with a morbid curiosity, other times with just a passing fancy, we want to know about the lives of others, so that we can better understand and accept our own reality.

I have also come to believe that above and beyond the curiosity to understand and accept ourselves, there is a prevailing, instinctive motivation that exists in each and every one of us…. and that is the quest for happiness, not fleeting happiness, but the kind of happiness that deeply satisfies the soul.

Janelle is a monthly client. For almost thirty years I have had the pleasure of enjoying her spunky, vivacious personality. Invariably, as she enters the front door, she announces, "I don't care what you do with my hair, just make me look ten pounds lighter." Other times she declares, "I don't care what you do with my hair. I just want to look rested and ten years younger when I leave." I feel confident in saying that the underlying feeling that Janelle wants from us is happiness.

Understandably, not everyone is conscious of the motivating factor that controls our activities, thoughts, and emotions—the desire to be happy. Most people don't take the time to think, "I'm acting badly, thinking destructively, and feeling emotionally tired because I am unhappy! I don't like my hair, so I'm unhappy. He disappointed me, and I'm unhappy, and now I'll make sure that he is unhappy. My mother never paid attention to me, so I'm depressed and unhappy; or my mother demands that I act a certain way, and if I don't, we will both be unhappy; or I need to have more money to be happy, and I am willing to kill for it." I believe that the desire for happiness is behind every action, thought, and feeling and can be the justification for the most heinous behaviors.

Many people live sad lives because happiness has not been encouraged in their formative years or accepted as a cause worth pursuing as adults. Instead, happiness has been demoted to a self-indulgent, unconscious accumulation of things and experiences that feed external and physical desires. Genuine, lasting happiness is a conscious act of being, which ultimately leads to the acceptance that life is meant to be a joyous expression of who we were created to be. We were created to be happy.

If all this desire for happiness sounds too shallow, dig deeper within yourself and discover your own motivation. What makes you get out of bed in the morning? Certainly not going to a job that you are unhappy doing. What makes you celebrate a special occasion? Could it be the excitement of accomplishing something that has brought you joy and happiness? Why do people take the risk of having surgery or taking noxious drugs to heal an illness? Perhaps it is the longing for an extended happy and healthy life. Why does anyone desire a home, car, children, perfect relationship, career, education, adventure, life purpose, or one of the most sought-after happinesses of all—financial freedom?

We are human beings who enjoy the physical, material world that surrounds us.... and why not? This is where we live! We were born to a physical existence.

Although I recognize that there are levels of our reality that include our mental astuteness, our emotional capabilities, and our spiritual connections, we will not be satisfied with what we accomplish outwardly unless we are first satisfied with ourselves inwardly. We must first establish happiness within ourselves at the emotional and spiritual level before we can express it in the material, physical world.

It is through our conscious ability to think that we can transform our external lives. The quest for finding happiness is actually the journey of becoming conscious of what it takes to make us happy. This journey can be a life-long adventure, or it can be the cause of a long-suffering life. The choice is ours to make.

Although this book is identified with the beauty industry, every business, event, person, and state of affairs can be a whole cosmos for learning to be happy. No matter what we are being or doing, we are creating stories for ourselves, developing patterns and perceptions of the way we view the world and the way we can be happy in it. These stories become our lives, and we share them with others as we strive to make sense of them.

We tell our stories, write about them, sing them, and share them electronically, but mostly, we continually create them through our daily lives. No matter where we've been, who we have become, or where we are going, we are living our lives and generating our stories. Finding happiness is a participation with everything else that exists, visible or invisible, and we are all connected and searching for the same result.

Within my beauty salon (the cosmic workplace of what's happening now) and in my personal desire for happiness, I have discovered several qualities that truly happy people embody. Please do not misunderstand. These people don't live in a protected bubble where only good happens, nor are they immune to sickness, death or disappointments; they simply know how to move through life with a discriminating responsiveness of how to make it work for them. No matter the circumstance, problem, or fear, they always regain their inner happiness and restore their outward happiness. And yes! Most of these people love their hair!

The First Quality Of Happiness Is Considerate
Awareness

Being considerately aware of another person, not just politely conversing but completely communing with interest, is the best gift that one person can give to another. Happy people participate fully in this experience by giving completely of themselves.

Elaine embodies this quality. During our many years together, we have developed a sincere appreciation for each other. Although our relationship has never left the boundaries of the hair salon, we have come to know each other as long-time friends who care about each other's happiness and well-being. I have always felt appreciated by her, and I have, in turn, valued her as a friend and client. During her monthly appointments, our discussions have been honest, humorous, and fascinating, mostly because Elaine rarely forgets anything. She remembers to ask about my newest project, my family, the outcome of my latest adventure, and, amazingly, she remembers stories that we discussed during other appointments. Considering her large family, network of friends, and work connections, I am positive that her ability to remember is due to her ability to be considerately aware in every situation and in every conversation.

Several years ago, at the age of seventy, Elaine was diagnosed with breast cancer. A few weeks into chemotherapy, her hair began to fall out by the handfuls. Instead of enduring the long and messy process of finding hair throughout the house, she decided to have it all shaved off. Cancer is what she had, and she was going to deal with it. Her plan for recovery was to be proactive with the medical treatments, to continue to eat healthy, to exercise, and to keep a positive attitude. She was not bemoaning, suffering, or trying to second-guess why it had happened to her, nor was she wishy-washy about her emotional state. Elaine was giving her cancer the complete awareness that it was demanding of her, and her expected outcome was a full recovery. Coming into the salon was one component of self-care toward her recovery.

That day in the salon, two other women were in various stages of hair color. As Elaine sat in my chair, I asked her permission to tell the other women what we were about to do. If one is not prepared to witness a mature woman having her thick, gorgeous, naturally dark hair shaved completely off her head, it can be a bit disturbing.

With a respectful voice, I explained to the women what was about to happen. As if someone had thrown a baby in the air and it was up to them to catch it, both women stepped quickly to Elaine and stood on either side of her and held her hands in theirs.

Strangers were sharing a difficult moment, not knowing the outcome, but acknowledging a soulful time together in considerate awareness for Elaine. They held hands quietly as I took the clippers to her perfectly round head. Automatically, the three women closed their eyes as Elaine's hair dropped to her shoulders, on to her lap, and then to the floor. In less then five minutes, it was over. Still holding hands, they opened their eyes.

Looking in the mirror and seeing herself bald for the first time, Elaine proclaimed, "And there I am!"

Laughter broke out in the room, and the spell that had originally held us in sorrow now set us free. At that moment, Elaine's years of considerate awareness toward others came full circle, and, in spite of the circumstances, everyone in the room felt the presence of shared happiness.

The Second Quality Of Happiness Is A Healthy
Sense Of Humor

I emphasize *healthy* in this quality because making fun of people's handicap and exploiting someone's shortcomings is not what happy people find humorous.

Happy people stay positive, no matter what happens. They see the humor in people's actions and reactions, and somehow they find the joy and the reward in the total human experience.

Hillary is a happy woman. No matter what time of day, day of the week, or month of the year that she walks into the salon, we smile when she enters. She is not the bearer of great jokes nor does she appear funny. She simply has a sense of enjoyment about life in general. As a social worker with children in the elementary school system, Hillary is an amazingly positive woman. She is also a wife, mother, and devoted daughter. In her free time she reunites adult adoptees and their birth parents through the Confidential Intermediary Program.

Without disclosing names or classified information, I have been privy to some extraordinary tales of reunions. Remarkably, her clients seem to be the most unusual sorts of characters...the most unlikely to be found, and yet through her tenacious research and jovial manner, she extracts entire life histories from complete strangers and gets the job done. Although the stories have been interesting and entertaining, the most enjoyable part of listening to Hillary has been the obvious happiness that she derives from her ability to help others. Countless people have been profoundly touched by her work, and, I venture to say, they have felt her optimistic view of life. I've watched and studied her over the years and have deduced that she anticipates experiencing humor in life...and she does.

In her personal life, an example of her light-heartedness is the story that she shared about her oldest son on his first day of driving alone. As the story goes, her son, after

176

proclaiming his flawless driving abilities, got into the family car, buckled up, started the engine, and promptly backed into the garage door, ripping it from its hinges. Most parents would have gone into a state of rage, but not Hillary. Aside from the consequence of having her son help pay for a new garage door and the damaged car, Hillary was relieved to have the first ding to the family car out of the way... and so close to home!

The Third Quality Of Happiness Is Admiration For The Physical Body

How many of us take the time to really study and appreciate the incredible work that the body does to keep us alive? If you have ever been physically compromised where the simple act of breathing became the miracle that kept you alive, you understand the word *admiration* in relation to the physical body.

Unfortunately, few and far between are the people whose high regard for their abundant lives has been credited to the health of their physical bodies. The majority of bodies have been dismissed as skin-bags, useful only as temporary carriers of thoughts, feelings and spiritual deeds. I'm sure you've heard it said, "I am a spiritual being having a physical experience." Meantime, the body is neglected and left to deal with distorted obsessions or dangerous addictions, obvious reactions to being disconnected and abandoned.

Conversely, when a person treats his body with a sense of admiration, it responds equally and returns the favor.

Doug, eighty-four years young, has high regard for his physical body. Although he is retired from farming, he continues to be extremely involved as a husband, father, grandfather, avid baseball enthusiast, and hobbyist. Nothing gets in the way of his daily walks and his heart-smart diet. His intent is to care for his body in return for the great life that it has given him. The majority of people that I talk to, like Doug, who are proactive about the care and maintenance of their bodies, have the same intention. They do not necessarily want to live forever, but to be healthy while they are alive. Doug's handsome, strong body is a reflection of a man who has spent his life aware of keeping his body well and happy.

When I asked Doug at what age he realized the importance of taking care of his body, he answered with a smile. "During high school I had three majors: baseball, basketball, and farming. It took energy, perseverance, and dedication to keep up with things around the farm, at school, and in sports. I had to learn how to eat, when to eat and what not to eat to keep myself strong. I began to appreciate what my body could do with the right attention. I was in awe of what I was capable of doing. From those early years, through respecting and caring for myself, I understood the responsibility and value of good health."

Seventy years later, what Doug learned about himself as a young athlete he still applies to his daily life. He continues, "Every *body* knows what it needs to be happy, and it has everything to do with what goes inside. What you eat and drink, how you move, and even how you think, matter. You have to keep your body happy from the inside out. It's that simple."

I have countless stories about clients who respect and listen to their body voice. They live fully with the ability to enjoy travel, spontaneity, adventure, and sexuality. They have the energy to experience life abundantly. The body will give back at the same level to which it is given. Or as my gym buddies say, "If you don't use it, you lose it."

Ask yourself this question: If your body could talk, what would it say?

The Fourth Quality Of Happiness Is
Unwavering Faith

People who have sincere and steadfast faith are absolutely, outrageously happy. They are not necessarily religious people who attend their church, temple, or mosque daily, nor do they go door to door trying to convert others, nor are they selective spiritualists who call upon God only when they need something. Rather, they are the committed ones who believe in a Divine Presence and a Divine Plan—all of the time.

Mrs. Woods holds a place in my heart as the most faithful and devoted person of all time. As a client for over thirty years, she never wavered from her complete trust that a Divine Presence had a handle on the great plan of her life, of the lives of her family and friends, and of the entire world. To her, nothing happens without God.

Once, during an appointment, having a conversation about her confidence in God, she admitted that faith was something to be continually worked on. She explained, "When things don't go our way, that is the time we are being tested. We have to be strong to make it through life and these tests are an exercise to strengthen our faith. I also think God has a sense of humor in the way He teaches us, and sometimes His tests are confusing, but we can still enjoy life as we learn to be more faithful."

She continued, "I remember once when my husband and I visited New York during the springtime, just before Easter Sunday. I thought I would treat myself to a New York hair salon and have a shampoo and set. My hair has always been white, and I was used to getting those rinses to keep it from turning yellow. As you know, all those rinses have either a blue or purple tint to them. I specifically said to the hairstylist to not leave the rinse on too long or it would grab the tint. Well! You can imagine what my husband said when I walked out of the salon *Easter egg blue.*

"We didn't have time for me to go back in and have it washed out, so we just made it a fun adventure in New York. Everywhere we went, my husband could spot me a mile away, and everybody talked to us. They might have felt sorry for me, but I didn't really care. We had a wonderful time and made lots of new friends."

Always, always faithful, Mrs. Woods was loved and respected by everyone who knew her. Her friendships ranged from the very young to those almost her age. Clearly, everyone recognized her sincere devotion and religious convictions and her unwavering relationship with God.

Before she passed away, I asked Mrs. Woods why she was always so happy (in her late eighties, living alone, still driving a car and playing tennis). She answered, "I have nothing to worry about. Why should I question God's love and direction for me?"

The Fifth Quality Of Happiness Is The Ability To Have Meaningful Relationships

I heard a successful salesman say that he never considered himself in the business of selling. Instead, his business was about forming relationships, uncovering the needs of his clients, and concentrating on giving instead of getting. That man was a smart salesman!

There are many reasons to form relationships, not just for selling someone something. The most fundamental motivation for connecting with others is basic survival. It is better and surely easier to unite to survive than to go it alone. After all, there is the matter of reproduction, and there is certainly strength in numbers. But beyond the primary instinct for continued existence, the goal to have meaningful relationships is icing on the cake of life.

Happy people develop meaningful relationships throughout their entire lives. Having been privy to hundreds of people's personal life stories, I am convinced that those who connect with others and share their lives are happier than those who don't.

This by no means suggests that only people who have many friends are happy. Meaningful relationships are not about quantity but about quality. It's about sharing adventures, trials, accomplishments, disappointments, life passages, and what we fear or love with someone who we think cares about us.

Many of my clients have reaped the benefits of being in meaningful relationships. Ed and Patti exemplify a couple who have spent their lives cultivating close, significant relationships. They have traveled extensively, experienced fascinating cultures, and explored the wonders of the world. All of this they have shared with others.

Most likely, not all of their relationships have been easy and pain-free. Like any other couple, there have been people who have come into their lives for a short time and others who have lasted the entire thirty-five years of their marriage. Nonetheless, they are happy people who enjoy meaningful connections.

Being a hairstylist has it benefits. Both Patti and Ed like my haircuts so much that during the summer months they fly me to their home in Washington State to do their hair. Last year, I flew in to attend Ed's eightieth birthday celebration. Because the Country Club could hold only one hundred guests, only their closest hundred friends and family members were invited to attend. I was delighted to make the cut.

Although the music, food, and entertainment were enjoyable, the best part of being there was witnessing the camaraderie and genuine caring that their friends showed for Ed and Patti. It was a wonderful display of the value that meaningful relationships bring to people's lives.

On several occasions, I have had the opportunity to ask Ed questions about his success in his business. His answer is always the same, "I'm a happy guy, Hilda, and I enjoy helping people get what they want."

P.S. Ed has been in sales all his life.

The Sixth Quality Of Happiness Is The Attitude Of Gratitude

I took my eyesight for granted until I could no longer see my face in the mirror to apply mascara. I didn't appreciate my hearing until I developed the ringing in my ears that distracts me from falling asleep at night. I thought I was overweight and complained about my body when I was in my twenties and thirties until now in my fifties my waist is as wide as my hips. At times my family embarrassed me because I thought we took first prize for the most dysfunctional family in the *world* until I came to view them as a cast of unique characters adding interest to my life at the most unexpected moments. I never realized how healthy I was until I wasn't. I protested against my boss's inability to lead until I became a boss myself.

Thinking back on the trillions of thoughts that I have created my life, I wonder how it might have been different had I been more grateful for what I had instead of wishing for something different. Truly, the most happy, satisfied, peaceful, triumphant people are those who discover the seed of gratitude in every circumstance in their lives.

I met Mark at a lecture that we both attended. Two weeks later, he came in for a hair appointment and admitted that I reminded him of his former wife. He described her simply as being my size with the same color eyes and the same color and length of hair. I didn't dare tell him that this was not my natural shade of auburn. If he stayed long enough with me as a client, though, he would find out for himself.

At his next appointment, Mark began telling me about his marriage of twenty years and his subsequent divorce. They were both in their late thirties when they met. They married within six months of a whirlwind courtship. It was her "free spirit" and exotic flair that initially attracted him to her. Her love for art, music, people, and sex launched Mark into new aspects of living that he had never experienced before. Mark, an engineer by trade, compulsively organized by nature, skeptical about everyone, and detailed in every way, found her exciting personality seductive. Within a few short months of their wedding, he knew it was going to be a lot more work than he had expected marriage to be. After all, they had lived alone as adults for many years, developing their own lifestyle preferences and establishing solid routines.

Mark traveled for work and had been with the same company since his graduation from college. Loyal, and concerned about his financial security, he justified doing the same thing for the rest of his career. His wife, on the other hand, worked in sales and stayed in a job until the next fun store or art gallery lured her away. Passionate about her connection to family and friends, she filled her extra time visiting, shopping, and going places with girlfriends.

As they worked on being together, each one learned to deal with the other's idiosyncrasies. Compromises were made, like house cleaning, which she did not enjoy doing. Instead, they hired a housekeeper who came in once a week. They also hired a gardener and an ironing woman, and when they stayed home for dinner, she cooked and he cleaned the kitchen.

There was one annoyance that Mark could not compromise about. Her hair.... it was all over the place. Mark found her thick, wavy, long, auburn hair everywhere. It drove him crazy. He found it in the shower drain, in the bathroom sink and countertop, and sometimes on their bed pillows. As he expressed his displeasure, she protested, claiming that he was obsessively out of line. After all, it was only hair, and it was natural to lose hair daily. Because he was almost bald and kept his hair very short, his hair was unnoticeable. Although Mark admitted that he brought up the hair objection on a regular basis, he could not believe that she took it so critically.

One evening, arriving home from a five-day business trip, Mark found a letter and signed divorce papers on the kitchen table. The letter simply stated, "You will not find any more hair to complain about. The divorce papers are signed. Do not try to reach me. I am not coming back."

By now I had finished cutting Mark's hair, and we were standing outside the salon. Even though she had been gone for over a year, and the divorce had been final for at least a year, I could see by his posture and his moist eyes that her leaving still saddened him.

He continued. "I find myself wanting to find a trace of her in the house. I breathe in deeply at night while I lie in bed alone, hoping to catch a sent of the wildflower perfume that she loved wearing. I keep thinking that this is all a dream and that soon I will awaken and she will be there next to me. Mostly, I look for her hair. I would give anything to find her hair in my bathroom sink and counter top or on the shower floor or on my pillow. I would be grateful for even one hair."

Sometimes we don't enjoy the best parts of our lives because we can't get past what we are *not* enjoying. If we could begin with the end in sight (to be happy) and flow with our circumstances instead of fighting them (suffering), we would naturally become grateful.

Each and every circumstance is part of the learning, growing, building progression of self-actualization. There are no wasted thoughts, emotions, words, or energy. All of it is useful and usable. The sooner we understand the value of every experience, the sooner we become grateful. Happiness naturally flows for those who are grateful.

When I told several colleagues that I was writing a book about the beauty industry, they all volunteered to give me their stories. Of course, there were plenty of horror stories about difficult clients, hair gone bad, salon disasters, and nightmare co-workers and bosses, but I had plenty of those of my own. Although the story about delivering a baby in a hair salon was tempting, what I actually appreciated most about our conversations was how many said they were grateful for their career as cosmetologists.

The beauty industry is a unique place to be. Just think about it! Everyone has hair—well, almost everyone. People need hair care. No matter the world conditions, economic climate, political posturing, or social habits, hair grows, and it needs attention. So far, it is one of the few services that has not been outsourced to another country. The industry continues to flourish.

Not long ago I read an article about a study of the happiest people in the workforce. According to the *Scottish News*, "Forty percent of hairdressers are happy in their chosen careers. The rest of the workforce is lagging far behind. Even among the clergy, who came in second to hairdressers in the poll, just twenty-four percent say they are happy. Could this mean that people will confide in their hairdresser rather than their pastor?" My experience says they do.

Recently, a friend gave me a small inspirational booklet written by Julio Melara. The booklet is titled *Keys to Performance*, and it contains a collection of one hundred keys and insights on topics that affect the performance, productivity, prosperity, potential, and possibilities in one's life.

This is what he says about Happiness: "Happiness is basically feeling good about yourself. Don't confuse happiness with popularity, which means that others feel good about you. What you think about yourself, your character and your own accomplishments determine your real sense of worth and value. There are two elements vital to your happiness—your relationships and your achievements. Life was never meant to be an endurance of trials, but an enjoyment of triumphs and accomplishments. And the best part of life, particularly if you live in America, is that you get to decide! Too many people look to someone else to bring them happiness. They are looking for material things and external solutions to an internal problem. Happiness does not start around you. It begins inside you!"

And as for me, "**Color Me Happy!**"

Hilda Villaverde

185

Other Books by Hilda Villaverde

Living on the Other Side of Fear: *A Spiritual Passion for Life*

Conscious Eating: *Prayers, Blessings, and Affirmations*
Hilda Villaverde and Friends

Women Inspiring Women: *A Journal for Remembering*
Hilda Villaverde and Angella Hamilton

Integrating Native American Teachings With New Thought Principles: *Journey Around the Sacred Circle and the Seven Directions to Peace*

Email Orders: www.hildavillaverde.com

Fax Orders: 480-657-9355 Phone Orders: 480-922-9315

Price per book: $19.95 Wholesale prices available for orders over ten (Please call to place order)

U.S. Shipping and Handling: Please add $5.50 for first book and $3.00 for each additional book mailed to the same address.

International Shipping and Handling: Please add $11.00 for first book and $6.00 for each additional book mailed to the same address. (Wholesale book sales will be mailed book rate, price adjusted.)

Sales Tax: Please add 8% for books shipped to an Arizona address. Credit cards accepted: Visa & MasterCard

Mail Orders:

Make Checks Payable to:
 Pluma Designs Inc.
7000 E. Shea Blvd. Suite 1614
Scottsdale, AZ 85254

Or you can order from:
www.hudsonhousepub.com or amazon.com